If You Had Stayed

JESSICA MADDEN

For my mum, the strongest person I know

Chapter 1

I stare at the numbers in my maths textbook. I don't know how long I have been staring at them. Nothing on this page made any sense to me, just a bunch of numbers all put together to make things complicated and confusing. I always had trouble understanding maths. Sometimes I wish I didn't choose it as one of my subjects for Year Eleven and Twelve. But it wasn't like I had a choice, as it's a compulsory subject for the HSC just like English. Plus, I needed it if I wanted to get into teaching. Not only couldn't I understand what the questions were about, but I also couldn't concentrate with the loud rock music coming from next door.

I set my pen down on my textbook and glance over next door. I see Josh sitting on his bed. He sat there still, processing whatever is going through his head. He is probably hearing the voices in his head again, and he was using the music to drown them out.

Joshua Harman has been my neighbour since we were nine. Our bedrooms look right into each other's. Being an only child, I was so happy when I learned he was moving in next door. We became friends instantly. After his parents died in a car accident, he was adopted by this nice couple who I have known since I was a baby. For years they have been trying to have kids, but weren't able to. Josh and I did everything together.

Two years ago, Josh's behaviour began to change. He had trouble sleeping, and it caused him to fall behind in school from his sleepless nights. I didn't really think of it at the time that there was something going on with him when he would drift off into space, where he wouldn't pay attention to what you might be saying or he wouldn't give you eye contact. He acted paranoid at times, fearing someone was coming for him. It should have been the first sign to notice something was wrong, but I passed it off like nothing was wrong. Or maybe I just didn't fully understand what was going on at the time. And then there was the voices. The voices were so loud that he claimed listening to music was one way he could control the voices he heard, as well as learning to play the guitar. But it couldn't control the hallucinations. He hid these things from everyone for a long time, even from me and I'm his best friend. We always told each other everything, but for this, Josh couldn't tell me.

It wasn't until last year when it became clear about his behaviour. He had an episode at school, screaming in the middle of the classroom, saying that someone was coming for him, ready to kill him. He switched off the lights in the room and closed the blinds and moved a table to block the closed door, telling us to hide him so the person couldn't find him. That day of his psychotic break, I have never seen him so petrified. He was then diagnosed with schizophrenia. Josh didn't tell anyone because he didn't know what was going on within himself, and he was afraid that I would stop being friends with him. I told him it was never going to happen. We will always be friends no matter what.

After a few minutes, the door to Josh's room opens, and his mother Lynn walks in. The window is closed, but I can hear her shouting at Josh to turn down the music. I watch Josh carefully, his fringe falling into his eyes as he shakes his head, arguing back at Lynn. She crosses her arms across her chest, scolding him once more. Finally, Josh drags himself off the bed and takes his phone out of the speaker dock, the music shutting off. Lynn says something else and then leaves Josh alone in his room.

He sits on the edge of his bed for a moment before looking over at me through the window. He smiles when he sees me. Getting up, he walks over to his window and opens it, climbing onto the tall tree that stood in between our homes. I get up from my desk and open the window. I shiver briefly as I let the cool winter air come in.

"Hey, Josh," I greet him as I help him inside.

"Can you believe Lynn told me to turn off the music?" Josh says instead of returning the greeting. He shakes his head. "I don't think Lynn or Phillip understands why I listen to the music so loud. It helps to drown out the voices, to distract me from it."

I closed the window. "Maybe don't play it so loud, or you could play your guitar. That should be good enough, right?"

Josh shrugs. "Maybe. Sometimes I don't know if I trust Lynn and Phillip."

"What do you mean, Josh?"

"I feel them judging me. Like why did they adopt me if I'm

going to grow up to be crazy? I can't help but feel they want to send me away so they don't have to deal with me."

I rest a hand on his shoulder and give him a small smile. Sometimes Josh tells me what the voices tell him, how he feels someone is out to get him, or his adopted parents want to send him away, not wanting to deal with him anymore. He views everyone as a potential enemy, except for me. He always feels safe around me, like I would protect him from others. I'm sure, though, that all of this is just a delusion, and no one is his enemy. "It's okay, Josh. No one is going to send you away."

"You don't know that, Emily." I see the fear in his deep brown eyes and I wish I could somehow take away the fear.

"For as long as I'm with you, Josh, no one will hurt you, and they won't be taking you away. I'll make sure of that."

I smile at him and he returns it, which causes my heart to do a somersault.

I turn back to my desk so I could continue my homework. The numbers in the textbook taunt me. I sigh with frustration as I ran my hands through my brown hair, trying to figure out this stupid maths equation. Why is this subject so hard for me?

"I really hate maths," I say.

Josh stands beside me, looking down at my homework. He picks up my blue ink pen and began scribbling on my maths grid book, solving the equation I couldn't answer. He doesn't stop there. I watch him as he answers every question on the page. I had almost forgotten that he was a whiz when it came to maths. He struggles to pay attention in class sometimes, but I was surprised at how well he was at maths. He answers them all without stopping to think.

Why couldn't I be just as great at maths like Josh is? He made it look so simple.

He hands my pen back to me. I smile, taking the pen and thanking him for his help.

"Do you need help with anything else?" he asks me.

"No thanks, Josh." I set my pen on the desk and closed my book. "You pretty much completed my homework for me so thanks for that."

He smiles at me, his eyes glowing in the light. It made my heart skip a beat. Sometimes I wonder what Josh feels for me. It's often hard to know what he is thinking when he doesn't always display his emotions, or tell you how he is feeling. There are times when we are in the moment where it feels right to lean over and kiss him, but then I'm afraid he would get mad with me, not knowing if he shared the same feelings for me as I do with him. Like right now he is standing so close to me. My palms are sweating and it's not even hot in here. I wipe my hands on my pyjama pants. I could so easily stand up from the chair and wrap my arms around him, pressing my lips against his. But no, I couldn't. I just couldn't do it. Not if it meant losing him as a friend.

We stare at each other for what seemed like a long time until a knock came from my door, making us both jump. Josh throws himself to the floor and crawls under my bed so he doesn't be seen by one of my parents.

The door creaks open and Dad pokes his head in to check on me. I keep my focus on him and try and not to glance at my bed, not wanting him to see Josh under there. Josh was always welcome to come over and hang out in my room, just as long as I had my bedroom door open. It's not just because my dad didn't want me to be alone in the bedroom with a guy. It was out of precaution just in case Josh tried to do something to hurt me. But I knew Josh. Even with his mental illness, he would never hurt me.

"Hey, have you finished your homework?" Dad asks me.

I nod. "Yes, it's all done." *All thanks to Josh*, I silently added to myself. If it wasn't for him, I would still be trying to wrack my brain.

"That's good. Don't stay up too late."

"I won't."

Most likely I'm lying because I didn't know how long I will be up for. Not with Josh here. We will talk a bit before any of us decide to fall asleep. Josh will fall asleep last. He always does. He stays awake to watch over me, making sure nothing will happen to me, even when I assure him that I will be safe. I never expect him to watch over for me, but he chooses to do so.

Dad leaves the room. Once the door is closed, I get off my chair and kneel on the floor, peaking underneath the bed. Josh is still under the bed, lying flat on his stomach, waiting for me to tell him if the coast is clear.

I smile at him. "You can come out now. My Dad is gone."

"Will he be back?"

I shake my head. "I don't think he will be back. If he does, it's probably to make sure I'm not staying up too late."

Josh crawls out from underneath.

We sit down on the edge of my bed. I watch Josh as we sit there in silence. I notice him looking around in different directions of the room, and I wonder if his hallucinations are in here with him. His medication helps him to prevent from seeing them, but every now and again they appear, including the voices. He talks to me about them sometimes, like they are real people. Georgia is my favourite of Josh's hallucinations. She is a hopeless romantic, always saying positive things and assuring him that everything is okay and he doesn't need to be scared. He always tells me that Georgia says that I'm a lovely person. She makes me smile even when I can't see her and I know she isn't real. And there are other times where he keeps quiet about them.

"How are the hallucinations going?" I ask him. "I know you were put on some new medication. Do they help with the hallucinations?"

Josh nods. He turns to me, but doesn't quite look at me. "A little. They still appear every now and again, but most of the time I don't see them."

I smile at him. "That is great to hear, Josh."

"I'm so used to hearing voices and seeing things that sometimes when I don't have Georgia or Aspen there to talk to me, it feels lonely and quiet." Aspen is one of his other hallucinations. He is a washed-up former rock star who always has something negative to say. Josh talks about them the most than any of his other hallucinations.

I squeeze his hand. I can't imagine what it must be like inside his head. "Maybe when that happens, listen to some music to distract you from it, or maybe play the guitar."

Josh nods, this time meeting my eyes. "I will give that a go."

"We should get some sleep, Josh. We have school tomorrow."

Josh nods in agreement. "Can I sleep over here tonight?"

I smile. "You know you're always welcome to do so."

He returns the smile and then rests his head on my shoulder. We sit there in silence for a few moments before I packed up my homework, Josh watching my every move. I switch off the light and climb under the covers. Josh lies beside me on top of the covers, saying goodnight.

Chapter 2

I wake up the next morning to see Josh lying next to me, fast asleep. He looks so at peace that I almost don't want to wake him. I watch him sleep for a few minutes, wondering what he could be dreaming about.

Careful not to wake Josh as he sleeps on top of my blankets, I climb out of bed. I should wake him up so he can go back next door and get ready for school, but I thought I would let him sleep a little while longer. I grab clean underwear from my draws, along with my blue and white school uniform from the floor beside my desk. I glance back at Josh, who hasn't stirred, and sneak out of my room.

I came out of my room at the same time my mother had come out from hers, which was just down the hallway from mine. She was already dressed in her business suit, where she worked as an editor for a fashion magazine.

Mum smiles, greeting me before asking if Josh was here. Whenever Josh slept over, I would get dressed in the bathroom. Mum is okay with him sleeping over, but my dad doesn't really like him spending the night in my room. So I only hope he doesn't find him because I don't want to be in trouble first thing in the morning about why my best friend is sleeping in my room without consent.

I nod. "Yes, he is. He is still sleeping."

"Would you like me to call Lynn to let her know where he is?"

I shook my head. "It's okay, Mum. There's no need for you to do that. Josh will wake up soon."

"Alright. Don't let him sleep for too long. I don't want him to be in trouble for being over here when he should be next door getting ready for school."

"No worries, Mum."

Mum gives me a warm smile and then walks past me to head downstairs to make breakfast. I turn to my right to enter the bathroom.

I undressed out of my pyjamas and into my uniform. Once dressed, I make a quick visit to the laundry to dump my clothes in the washing machine before heading back to my room to check on Josh. He is no longer sleeping in my bed when I get there, which he had made neatly for me. He was now next door, the curtains in his room closed.

Smiling, I brush my hair and tie it into a ponytail before heading downstairs for breakfast.

* * *

My friend Haylie is waiting for me at the front of the school when Mum drops me off on her way to work. I greet her, making small talk as we wait for Josh to arrive. Mum had offered to drive both Josh and I to school together, but Lynn says she doesn't mind taking him and didn't want it to be a hassle for Mum. Lynn often had trouble getting Josh to leave for school, where he would make a fuss every morning about how much he hated it. I don't blame Josh for not wanting to go. Ever since our grade found out about his psychotic break, he was bullied by some students for being crazy. Some teachers look at him in a different way too, like they fear he would become dangerous, but Josh wasn't anything like that. Yet, a majority of the school still treated him normally like any other student here.

"So have you booked your test yet?" Haylie asks me, her shoulder-length blonde hair hangs loose, blowing slightly in the cold breeze.

I nod excitedly. "I'm going for my licence on Friday after school."

Haylie returns the excitement, beaming as she high-fives me. "Awesome. Are you excited or nervous about it?"

"I'm a bit of both. I'm trying not to be too nervous or I know I will fail the test."

"You won't fail, Emily. I have faith in you. And just imagine when you do pass, you will no longer be on your learner's and you can go anywhere you want to go."

I often wonder where I'll go once I get off my learner's and no longer have to drive with a full-licence driver. I thought of taking Josh somewhere with me. I imagine us going on road trips and exploring Australia someday once we graduate at the end of the year. Haylie and I had also discussed that maybe the three of us could go on a trip together for the Christmas/New

Year break, to celebrate the end of high school.

I was about to agree with Haylie and tell her the plans I wanted to do, when I saw a black hair girl walking towards us from our left. Gabrielle Casey, the biggest bitch in our grade. I despise her more than anything in the world. She prefers to be called Gabby rather than by her birth name. She got everything she wanted and never let anyone stand in her way. Gabby is also a teacher's pet.

As she approaches us, I notice the tiara on top of her head that had HAPPY BIRTHDAY on it in sparkling sliver glitter letters. Her arm was linked around her boyfriend, Lake Terra. He didn't look please about something and I wouldn't blame him. I wouldn't be happy either if I had Gabby as my girlfriend.

Gabby spots Haylie and I, strolling over to us with a smirk on her face, which I wanted to wipe off badly. Better yet, I wish she would disappear off the face of this planet. I didn't need her to come over to us and start saying nasty stuff about Josh like she always does, like she is better than everyone else because she doesn't suffer from a mental illness and isn't considered "crazy" like Josh is.

"Hi there, Haylie. Emily." The way she paused before she said my name was like she wasn't pleased to see me or it was her way to warm up to her insults. "Waiting for Freak, I see." She laughs at her own comment.

I clench my jaw, wanting to pound Gabby's face in with every chance I have. Ever since word got out about Josh's illness, never once did she call him by his proper name. Freak was the main insult she called him by. Not only her, but some other students in our grade call him that too, all thanks to her who started the whole name calling. It tears my heart to pieces to hear how cold-hearted she can be towards someone, especially when they are different. But to me Josh is still a human being, even if he has a mental illness that makes him lose touch with reality. It doesn't mean you have to treat them differently, right?

Haylie could see it in my face of what I wanted to do to Gabby. If it wasn't for the school rules, I probably would have punched Gabby's face in already, just to wipe the smile off her face. Gabrielle Casey wasn't worth getting detention.

"He has a name, you know," Haylie speaks for me. "It's Josh."

"It is?" Gabby looks at us like she was just learning about his name for the first time. "I really thought it was Freak considering he is crazy. The name suits him well."

I frown at her. "Having a mental illness doesn't make him a freak, Gabby. He is still a human being. He just... He has just lost touch with reality."

"Whatever. He is still a freak anyway. He shouldn't even be here. He belongs in some psychiatric ward, locked up in a room with a straitjacket."

I shake my head. "No one deserves that, Gabby."

Gabby rolls her eyes, clearly not giving a care in the world to what I had to say. "Anyway, it's my birthday." She points to her tiara with a big smile. "I'm having a birthday party tonight for my eighteenth. It's going to be big. I don't really want to invite you two, but my parents thought it would be good if I invite everyone in our grade. And if you reject the invitation, I will make your life hell."

Haylie raises her eyebrows at her. "Gabby, you already make our life hell."

Gabby throws her a dirty look before returning it to a happy and smiley one. "You're both invited. And if you do decide to come, don't you dare bring Freak."

I frown at her. "Why can't he come? I mean, he is in our

grade too."

I knew the answer already. Gabby didn't even have to give it to me. But I wanted her to say what she really thought to my face. I wanted her to tell me instead of telling it to Josh because he doesn't deserve to be treated like some outcast just because he was different. It's not his fault for his illness, and I just wished that no one held it against him. They shouldn't, but some people just want you to feel bad.

Gabby laughs like what I said was one big joke. Lake doesn't laugh as hard as his girlfriend, but it was more of a smirk.

"Are you seriously asking me that question?" Gabby says. "Please, even if Freak was the last person on earth, I wouldn't invite him." She turns to Lake. "Come on, babe. Let's go."

Haylie and I watch as Gabby walks away with her boyfriend, whose arm, was still linked around hers.

"Are you going to go to her party?" Haylie asks me once Gabby was out of earshot.

I shake my head. Was she kidding? She knows very well that I would never go. "Why would I after the way she speaks about Josh?"

Haylie nods. "True, it isn't right. But listen..." She bites her lip. "I might go to it. Well, I may go if I find out that Jensen is going to it."

Of course that would be the reason why she would attend Gabby's party. She had been crushing on Jensen Peters for a while.

"If he is coming," Haylie continues, "would you come with me, Emily? You know, just to be at my side. But if things don't work out with Jensen or if the party gets boring, we can leave."

"I will think about it, Haylie. If I don't have too much homework, I will go."

I didn't have the heart to tell her that I wasn't interested in going, especially to a party where someone despised Josh. Besides, I wanted to stay home and maybe do something with him tonight. I know he has been working on some new music that I thought he could play for me on his guitar.

Just thinking about Josh, I see Lynn's Honda pulling up to the kerb. Josh was in the front seat, arguing with her about the music from last night.

"Honey, I understand, but there is no reason for you to listen to it that loud," Lynn was saying.

"No, you don't understand. It helps me to block out the voices."

Lynn pats his shoulders. "I know it does, Josh, and I want you to know that I won't stop you from listening to it. I'm just saying to lower the volume next time."

Josh takes a deep breath and nods. He unbuckles his seat belt. "Okay."

He opens the door as Lynn tells him to have a good day. She smiles at Hailey and I. She winds down the window just as Josh closes it and stands beside me.

"Hello, Hailey, Emily," she greets us.

"Hello, Lynn," we greet her back.

"Have a good day, girls."

She closes the window and then pulls away from the kerb.

"How are you today, Josh?" I ask.

He smiles. "I'm good."

"Everything okay between you and Lynn?"

He nods. "Yeah, we are okay. You know, just talking about my music."

The three of us head inside the school grounds. The bell was due to ring in ten minutes. We weren't allowed inside the building until the bell rings, so we head to our favourite spot to sit in the mornings before school started. Sometimes we even had lunch there. As we walk, I notice Josh looking in different directions and I wonder what hallucinations he was seeing today. He was quiet this morning and I hoped he was feeling okay.

We reach our favourite spot near the front entrance of the administration office and outside the visual arts classrooms, sitting down on the seat underneath the tree. Thankfully no one is sitting there this morning, and I'm glad. It's a place the three of us can sit and relax before school started. The tree was the perfect shady place during the summer. It wasn't so great for the winter months, but it was a place we liked to hang and talk. For Josh, nature often calms him when he is feeling anxious, and sitting under the tree was something he liked to do.

"Did you guys end up completing the homework Mr Carlson gave us?" Haylie asks us as she place her bag on her lap.

Josh nods as he sat down beside me, setting his bag down beside his feet. "I did. It was a piece of cake."

I scoff, resting my bag on my lap. "Of course it was a piece of cake for you. You're a whiz at maths." I turn to Haylie. "I kind of completed it."

She raises an eyebrow. "What do you mean kind of?"

"Well, I didn't really do it. Josh did it for me. He came over last night and saw me struggling with my work, and he answered them for me. The amazing thing is he didn't even stop to think what the answers were. He just answered them with no trouble at all."

Haylie looks over at Josh in surprise. "What's your secret, Josh? How can you do maths so well?"

Josh shrugs. "There's no secret. I'm just good with numbers."

Haylie turns to me. "Did he get all of the questions right?"

I nod. "I looked up the answers in the back of the textbook and they are all correct."

"Wow, that's incredible. You just hope Mr Carlson doesn't think you cheated."

I chuckle. "I doubt it. I'm pretty sure half of the class actually do look up the answers in the back without working it out for themselves, and he doesn't say anything."

"He will know you looked them up when you do your tests and can't work out a single thing the paper says, but yet you can answer them correctly in your maths book."

Haylie had a point. "True. But whether I do it the right way or not, I still suck at maths."

"Hey, Freak!"

We look up to see Elliot Cox walking over to us with his friend Ron Gold. Their eyes were set on Josh. Josh sees them, getting up to swing his bag over his shoulder, ready to make a dash if he needed to. The guys didn't even seem to care that Haylie and I were sitting right there beside him. Haylie and I stood just as Elliot and Ron approach him, grabbing him by the shoulders before he had a chance to escape and push him into the tree trunk. Both of the boys were slightly taller than Josh.

"Elliot, Ron, stop it," I scroll at them.

But they act like I'm not even there.

Josh tries to push them off him, but the boys don't let go of him, keeping him pin up against the tree.

"Hey, Freak, seen anything that shouldn't be there lately?" Elliot smirks.

I approach Elliot and Ron, and as I put my hands on their shoulders, Josh looks to his right where I'm sure he was probably seeing Davis, the bad boy who is always ready to get into a fight and protect Josh from anyone who tries to threaten him. He shouts out, "No!"

The tone of his voice makes me jump for a brief second, making me take a step back in case he was protecting me from something I couldn't see. Ron and Elliot just laugh.

"Who are you talking to, Freak?" Ron laughs.

I put my hands on Ron, not even sure if Davis was still here, even though there was nothing he could do to stop these two bullies from hurting him. But I could do a whole lot more than what Josh's hallucinations could. And if they were real people, I'm sure no one would mess with Josh.

I push Elliot out of the way so I was standing in between him and Ron. "Leave him alone."

Both Ron and Elliot let go of Josh and turn to me.

"Maybe I don't want to leave him alone," Elliot says.

"Well, I'm telling you to leave him alone. You have no right to come over here and start causing trouble."

Elliot smirks, standing right up in my face. I take a step back. "Oh yeah? What are you going to do about it if I don't leave him alone?"

I point towards the school building. "Leave Josh alone, or I will march right to the principal's office to report you." I put my arm back at my side. "I don't think you want to be called down to Mr Mathison's office first thing in the morning for bullying another student."

Elliot's jaw clenches. "You aren't going to do that, you hear me?"

I glare at him, his brown eyes threatening mine. I wasn't going to let this bully stand in the way of my best friend.

I turn towards Josh and Haylie. "Come on, Haylie, Josh. Let's go."

I go to turn, but Elliot grabs my wrist.

"Hey, I didn't say you could walk away from me. You think you're Josh's hero?" He laughs. "Trust me, Emily, but you need to stay away from this freak. He is dangerous. He's mental. He belongs in a straitjacket."

I shake my head, pulling my arm around him. Before I had a chance to defend myself, Josh grabs Elliot from behind.

"Don't you dare touch, Emily," Josh warns. He drops his arms at his side and stares at Elliot, ready to fight him if he needs to.

"And what are you going to do about it if I do touch her?" Elliot puts his face right up to Josh's.

Josh looks at me and then shoves Elliot hard in the chest to get him away. Ron steps forward, but I see the panic in Josh's face as he takes a step backwards. Josh wasn't a fighter or believed in any kind of violence. Some students at this school, maybe even some of the teachers, feel he is a violent person just because he has schizophrenia. Teachers always kept a close eye on him in case he harms other students, but Josh has never done that to anyone. Not even to me. If he wanted to hurt anyone, it would be himself. Ron and Elliot, always provoked him in hoping Josh will do something crazy, or do whatever myth people might believe that someone with schizophrenia was capable of doing.

Before the boys could get into an out of control fight, which is the last thing I wanted because I knew Josh will immediately be blamed, Haylie and I step in between them. Haylie scolds at them both to leave Josh alone, while I walk Josh away.

"Are you okay, Josh?" I ask him.

"I'm fine," he says.

I look over my shoulder to see Hailey walking over to us. Elliot and Ron were laughing, probably saying something about Josh. I don't know how they can be proud of what they do. They should be ashamed. I was afraid they would follow us, but luckily the bell rings and we head inside to roll call.

Chapter 3

I doodle a heart in the back of my maths book, writing Josh's name inside it, barely paying any attention to what Mr Carlson was talking about. He was talking about Algebra, but my mind had drifted off as soon as he started talking about x and y, and how to find the answer which didn't make any sense to me at all. Why can't Algebra be simple? Why make it complicated by adding letters instead of numbers that could maybe make it easier to understand?

I smile at my drawing, not realising that Mr Carlson was watching me.

"Emily," he calls to me. My head shoots up in his direction, the smile fading away. "Is there something you would like to share with the class?"

My cheeks burn as I notice all eyes were on me. I shake my head. "No, Mr Carlson. There's nothing to share."

Mr Carlson watches me for a few seconds, like he was searching my face to see if I was telling the truth. He then nods. "Good. Please pay attention." He turns back to the whiteboard and starts scribbling on it. "Anyway, as I was saying..."

I ignore his request to pay attention. The whole time my teacher spoke, all I heard was "Blah, blah, blah..." How do I pay attention when that's all I can hear only because numbers and equations don't mean a thing to me?

I glance over at Josh, who sat beside me in the back row of the classroom next to the window. Josh was watching me with concern.

Making sure our teacher wasn't looking our way, he mouths, "Is everything okay?"

I nod, and mouth back, "I'm fine." I smile.

Josh returns the smile. He then turns back to his grid book to take notes.

Just as I turn to look back at my own work before I get caught not paying attention again, a scrunched up piece of paper lands in front of me. I glance up at Mr Carlson to make sure he didn't see anything, but his back was to me as he wrote on the board. Haylie, who is sitting beside me, watches me as I grab the paper, opening it without Mr Carlson seeing me. Haylie glances down at it and we read it silently together.

If you didn't hang around Freak too much, the note read, *then you wouldn't have that big goofy smile on your face. Be careful, Emily. You don't want to end up as a psycho like him.*

It wasn't signed by anyone, but I automatically knew who the note was from. I glance up, looking over at Gabby who was sitting one row up and two seats down from Haylie and me. She has a smirk on her face as soon as we make eye contact with her. I crunch the note in my hand, wanting to get up from my seat and wipe the smirk off her face. How dare she write something like this to me? Why doesn't she come over here and say it to my face?

Haylie puts her hand over mine. I look at her and she shakes her head. I was glad she was sitting next to me. The last thing I wanted was to get detention or be sent down to the principal's office. Gabby was not worth getting myself into trouble.

* * *

"Ignore what she wrote, Emily," Haylie tells me as the three of us walk to our next class. "All Gabby wants to do is make you mad."

It was easy for Hailey to say to just ignore it. The words Gabby had said about me and Josh in the note will keep playing in my mind, and it was something I'm glad Josh hasn't seen. I don't understand how Gabby can say so many nasty things. How would she feel if someone was to say it to her? How would she want people to treat her if she had a mental illness?

"I know, I know," I say. "It's just so hard to ignore the things she says about Josh."

Josh puts his hand on my shoulder. "Let her say what she wants to say, Em. In the end, at least you are kinder than Gabby will ever be."

I nod, knowing Josh was right. Gabby was never going to be a nice person. She doesn't even have respect for herself, so why would she have any respect for others? She probably mistreated others their whole lives. Or maybe she only became a bully when we started high school. In Year Seven, before Josh was even diagnosed with his illness, Gabby had treated us like a nobody from day one, like she could sense we were different and didn't want to be anywhere near us.

Haylie moves in closer to me, whispering in my ear so no one or Josh could hear. "Does Gabby know you have feelings for Josh?"

I shake my head. I couldn't imagine the things she would say if she knew about my crush on Josh. I whisper back, "No, she doesn't know, and I prefer she doesn't. You're the only person who knows."

"Hey, what are you two whispering about?" Josh asks us with a smile. "Am I'm not supposed to know?"

I turn to Josh, returning the smile. "It's just girl stuff. I don't think you would be interested."

"Well, okay. If you say so."

We reach our classroom. No one was inside yet and our classmates showed no interest in going inside, where they stood outside the room and chatted to their friends. I tell Josh to go in and take a seat so I could talk to Haylie without him hearing our conversation. I watch Josh walk into the classroom, taking a seat in the back row beside the window.

Haylie and I stood near the doorway. "I will never tell Gabby or anyone that I have a crush on him. I don't want to know what she will say if she ever finds out."

Haylie pats my shoulder. "I know. I can imagine all the insults Gabby will say if she knew. But don't worry about her finding out. Even if she did, she can't stop you from falling in love with whoever. Are you going to tell Josh eventually that you like him?"

I shrug. "Maybe. I want to."

"Then what's stopping you? You should tell him. I'm sure he will return the same feelings."

"And what if he doesn't?"

"What if he does?"

I look over at Josh. He had his book open, ready for class to start. Butterflies danced around my stomach, and I knew Haylie was right. I should tell him.

"I'm afraid he won't return the feelings," I say, turning back to Haylie. "What if he doesn't like me back and it ruins our friendship?"

"You won't know until you try, Emily." She gives me an assuring smile. "I'm pretty sure he likes you, too."

Haylie enters the classroom first. I stand there for a moment, thinking about what she had said. She was right. Maybe it was time to tell him how I felt, but I didn't know how to. There was still that fear of rejection that he may not feel what I feel. And once I get what I feel out there, would our friendship be the same even if he didn't share the same feelings?

* * *

During lunch I headed up to the music room while Hailey went to talk to a teacher about an assignment. Josh had decided he wanted to spend his lunch in the music room. Mrs Hartley often allows him up here during lunch, giving him a place to escape for the forty minutes of our lunch break.

I hear the guitar playing as I approach the room, where the door was opened. Josh sat on a table, his feet resting on a chair, as he strums a few chords on the instrument. I sit with him.

"That sounds good, Josh," I say.

He stops playing and looks up at me with a smile. "Thanks. It's this new song I have been working on."

"Oh cool. Can you play it for me?"

Josh bites his lip. "Uh, it's not quite ready."

"That's okay. I don't mind listening to what you have got so far."

Josh nods, and begins strumming the chords. Soft music plays and I sit there watching Josh play. He doesn't sing, just silently runs his fingers along the guitar strings as he concentrates. For a moment, I forget about where we are, as it's just the two of us in this room.

I think back to what Hailey told me earlier. It still makes me wonder what Josh will say if I confessed how I felt. I felt lost in his music, and all I wanted was to put my hand over his and turn his face towards me so I could feel his lips on mine. But it didn't feel like it was the right time to do so.

Not here where anyone could walk in and see us.

Tonight, I say silently to myself. *I will tell him tonight.*

* * *

I agreed to go to the Gabby's party with Hailey, even when I really didn't want to. But I promised her I would be there if she needed me in hope the guy she liked will take notice of her. Hailey said we will just stay there for an hour, neither of us really wanting to be at the party. Although I don't think we will be there for an hour, not when Haylie is shy when it comes to Jensen. The party was starting at five, and since it was a school night, it will be ending around eight. But if we do stick to our plan with staying for an hour, it was probably all the best as neither of us had gotten Gabby a birthday present, and there's no doubt she will be expecting something from us even if we aren't her friends.

Before I leave to meet Haylie out front, I carefully climbed onto the tree, swinging to the other side to see Josh. We had asked Josh to come with us, despite what Gabby had said earlier. But he declined our offer, wanting to stay in and work on the song he was playing at school earlier.

Josh is sitting on his bed when I came to the window, working on his homework as he listened to music. I tap on the window gently, careful not to startle him from the knocking. He glances up from his book and smiles at me, getting off the bed to let me in.

"Hi, Emily," he says, grabbing my hand and helping me into his room.

"Hey, Josh. What are you up to?"

"Nothing much. Just homework. I'm thinking of finishing up soon to work on the song I played earlier. I want to play it for you when you get back from the party."

I smile. "Well, I can't wait to hear it. Haylie and I shouldn't be at the party for too long. We are staying for an hour. Are you sure you don't want to come along?"

Josh shakes his head. "I'm sure. You have a good time, Emily."

He gives me a hug. With our arms wrapped around and our bodies pressed up against each other, I swear at that moment I wanted to ditch the whole party with Hailey. I wanted to stay here with Josh, and be wrapped up in his arms for the entire night. I wanted it to be just us tonight.

Josh rests his chin on top of my head, his fingers running through my hair. "Your hair is so soft and smells like coconut. Did you get a new shampoo?"

I pull away from him and nod. "I did."

"It smells nice. I like it."

"Thanks."

"So, you promise you will be back in an hour?"

I nod. "I will try to. Honestly, I feel this party is a waste of time and it's going to be a drag. But Hailey wants me to come in hope that Jensen Peters will be there."

"Is she planning to ask him out?"

"I hope so. She has been crushing on him for months, so hopefully tonight she will finally talk to him."

And you need to do the exact same thing, Emily, I tell myself. *Don't feel afraid to confess your feelings to him.*

"Emily?" I hear my mother's voice from my room.

I turn to see her walking in, searching for me. I wave at her through the window. "Over here, Mum."

She looks over at me and Josh, smiling. She walks over to my window so she doesn't have to shout from the doorway. "Haylie is here."

"Okay. Tell her I will be right down."

Mum says hi to Josh before leaving my room to pass my message onto Hailey.

I turn back to Josh. "I will see you later."

I give him another hug, as well as a kiss on the cheek and told him I will text him to when I was heading home. I climb back over to my house to head out to a party I was still dreading to go to.

Chapter 4

Like we had expected, Gabby's party wasn't all so glam up to be like she had told us it will be. And even though she had invited everyone in our grade sort of like last minute, only half of them bother to show up. To Hailey's disappointment, Jensen Peters did not show up to the party liked she had hoped.

The party was held in the backyard of Gabby's place. Fairy lights were decorated around the patio, and students dance to the music that's playing or stand around talking. There's a swimming pool, but no one is near the pool area on this cold night. There's no alcohol at this party as we have school the next day, and I'm pretty sure Gabby's parents are somewhere nearby, making sure no one does slip in any alcohol. Most of us are eighteen, but I'm sure no one is going to want to go to school tomorrow with a hangover.

Haylie and I stand beside the refreshment table, drinking

peach iced tea. We have only been here for half an hour and the party was already a drag for us.

"Hey, do you want to get out of here once we finish these drinks?" Haylie asks me.

I nod. "Yeah, I really don't want to stay any longer."

She gives me an apologetic smile. "Listen, Emily, I'm sorry for making you come along here with me. I should have known Jensen wasn't going to show up."

I put my hand on her shoulder. "Hey, don't blame yourself."

"I was really hoping he would be here and have a chance to talk to him."

"You will, Hailey. If you can't talk to him at this party, then try to talk to him at school. I will be right beside you when you do." I give her a smile.

Hailey returns the smile. "Thanks, Emily."

My phone began ringing from the pocket of my jeans. I pull it out to see who was calling. Lynn Hopkins. My body freezes when I see her name. She never calls me. My first thought is that something happened to Josh.

My finger slides across the screen to accept the call. I put my cup on the table and put the phone to my ear, while blocking out the noise with my finger in the other ear. In the background of the call, I hear screaming and panic in the person's voice. Josh. "Hello, Lynn?"

"No, you can't leave me here!" Josh screams in the background. "I don't want to be here!"

"Emily, hi," she answers. "I'm so sorry to have to call you. I know you're out right now, but is it possible you could come to the hospital?"

My body goes cold. "Why? What happened to Josh?"

"Phil found him unconscious in the bathtub. Thank

goodness Phil found him when he did and revived him." I hear her sniff. "Oh gosh, I can't believe Josh has gone and done this to himself. I'm sorry to stop you from doing whatever you're doing, Emily, but do you think you can come down here. Josh would really appreciate it if you come visit him."

Lynn's words slowly sink into me. I had a hard time believing what she was telling me because this was so unlike Josh. He has never tried to attempt suicide before. And right before I left his room almost an hour ago, he was fine. He showed no sign of wanting to take his life or showed that he was depressed. Often the negative voices would tell him to do things he knows he shouldn't or didn't want to do. He doesn't like talking about it, but he always feels safe to tell me, and of course he tells his psychiatrist, about the horrible things the voices tell him. Whenever he had those thoughts or just wanted to block out any kind of voice he was hearing, he turned to music in hope the voices would go away. His medication also helps him to control them.

But for whatever reason, Josh decided to listen to that negative voice this time.

I tell Lynn I will be at the hospital soon.

I hang up the phone, shaking all over from the news.

"Emily?" Haylie asks with concern.

I turn to her, slipping my phone into my pocket. My voice shakes as I speak. "We need to go. Josh is in the hospital."

Haylie puts her almost empty plastic cup on the table, letting the news sink in. "Is Josh okay?"

I tell her what had happened.

Haylie curses. "Come on, let's go. I will drive you there."

"Thanks, Haylie."

Haylie downs the rest of her drink, and leaves the empty

cup on the table. She leads the way, making our way through the crowded backyard to the side of the house where we hope to slip out through the side gate without being seen, especially by Gabby. I see her standing beside the pool fence gate talking with her friend Samantha.

Haylie opens the side gate, leaving the sound of the party behind us. We almost slip out of the gate when we hear a voice from behind us.

"Are you leaving now? We are going to be cutting the cake any minute. You should stay for it."

We turn to see Lake walking over to us, holding a can of Coke. Did he really just followed us here to tell us about Gabby's birthday cake that I really had no interest in right now?

"We would love to stay for cake," Haylie says, speaking for the both of us, "but we really need to go. See you in school tomorrow."

"Is everything okay?" Lake asks, concerned. He must have seen the worry on my face.

"Everything is fine," I answer. "I just need to get to the hospital."

Lake, of course, doesn't believe me. "Are you sure everything is okay? Do you need help with something?"

I shake my head. "No, I'm fine."

Lake nods. "Okay, well you better go before Gabby sees you. She won't like it if you leave."

I'm sure it won't be the end of the world if we leave, I wanted to say, but kept it to myself.

"Well, we never really got her a present," I say instead, "so I think she would be madder at that more than with us leaving."

"Yes, you're definitely right." He looks over his shoulder before turning back to us.

Haylie opens the gate and I follow behind her. Lake walks out with us. The three of us walk in silence down the street towards Haylie's car, leaving the sound of the party behind us. I glance at Lake a few times, not even sure why he was following us out here. I wanted to say something, but decided not to.

"Oh, you have got to be kidding me," Haylie says when we reach her car, which was parked two houses down from Gabby's.

All four tyres on her car were flat, and the front passenger side window was smashed. There were two empty beer cans on the grass beside the vehicle, which meant someone from our grade had been out here and vandalised it. So much for keeping the party clear of alcohol. Someone still managed to sneak it in.

"I think it might have been Elliot Cox and Ron Gold," Lake says. "I saw them leaving, and when they came back they were bragging to my friends and me about smashing someone's car. They didn't say whose car, but they did say they were getting someone back for something."

I sigh. Did those two have to be so immature only because Haylie and I stopped them from hassling Josh earlier today? There was no need for them to vandalise Haylie's property just because they couldn't get their way.

Haylie curses under her breath. "This is so going to cost me a fortune to repair."

"Why would they want to get you back?" Lake wants to know. Why was this guy out here with us? "What did you do to them?"

"Nothing. All Emily and I did was tell those idiots to leave Josh alone. They didn't have to go and seek revenge like this. Jerks."

Haylie opens the door. The light inside comes on and she climbs in.

"Is anything missing?" I ask her.

"No, they didn't take anything." Haylie looks over at me. "Sorry, Emily, but I don't think I can take you to the hospital. I'm going to call my dad to tell him what happened. Maybe he can drive you there so you can see Josh."

I shake my head. "No, it's okay. You don't need to get your dad to do it. I can just take an Uber there. Or maybe I will see if one of my parents can come get me."

"There's no need for you to go through the trouble of getting an Uber," Lake speaks up. "I can drive you."

I stare at Lake, wondering why he was being so kind to me and Haylie. I'm not saying it's a crime or anything, but he has never been this kind to us. He never even spoke to us. Gabby makes sure he doesn't. She controls him, treats him like a puppet and gets him to do her dirty work. She gets her friend Samantha to do the same thing. I don't know how he even lets Gabby treat her like that, or follows her everywhere like a lost puppy.

"That's okay." I give him a small smile. "You don't need to do that. Besides, don't you have to be with Gabby? She is not going to be happy you ditched her on her birthday."

"I'm not ditching her. I'm just helping someone out and I will be back here. She can survive for a minute without me. Seriously, Emily. It's no trouble at all for me to drive you."

I thank him, and decided to let him take me. At least it will save me some money getting the Uber.

I say goodbye to Haylie, feeling guilty that I was leaving her out here on her own, but she said she will be fine. I promised to let her know how Josh was later. I then follow Lake to his car, which was parked in the driveway of Gabby's home.

As Lake pulls onto the street, I pray silently to myself that Josh will be okay.

Chapter 5

"Thank you again for driving me," I say to Lake from the passenger seat.

"It's no problem," he replies. "Anyway, I was looking for a way to escape the party. So I should be thanking you for giving me a reason to leave. Gabby has been getting on my nerves lately, and I'm really starting to get sick of her bossing me around." He sighs, shaking his head. "Maybe I should consider breaking up with her."

I raise my eyebrows, surprised to hear him say this. I had always thought he enjoyed Gabby's company, but I guess I can't blame him for wanting to leave. And if he does decide to break up with her, I can imagine the trouble it will cause between the two of them.

"You're going to ask for war if you do."

Lake nods, keeping his eyes on the road. "I know. I'm prepared."

I stare out the window of Lake's car, watching our surroundings pass by, my throat tightening as we get closer to the hospital. I wonder about Josh and if he will be alright. I can imagine him when I walk into the room, his face will light up like a Christmas tree. He will hug me tightly, and tell me about whatever delusional thoughts he could have about the doctors and nurses. Maybe he will tell me what Georgia, Aspen, Davis and his other hallucinations may be doing. Or maybe we won't talk about any of that. Maybe he would just want to enjoy my company, someone he can feel safe with.

"So what's wrong with Freak?" Lake asks me, snapping me out of my thoughts. "Why is he in the hospital?"

I shoot him a filthy look. It is bad enough Gabby calls him it. I don't need to hear it from everyone else either.

"I mean, Josh," he quickly apologises when he sees the look I give him out from the corner of his eye. "Sorry. I'm just used to calling him Freak because Gabby calls him that."

"Just because Gabby calls him that, Lake, doesn't mean you have to say it too. His name is Joshua. No other name. I already hate Gabby for calling him that in the first place. How would you feel if everyone started calling you some kind of insult just because you have a mental illness? Do you think you're a freak if you had an illness like that? Or if you had a disability? Josh already hates himself because of his illness. It's rare to get schizophrenia before your early twenties, and all he wants to do is try to get through the rest of high school without being make fun of just because he is different to everyone else."

Lake doesn't answer straight away, just nodding. "I'm sorry. I won't call him names again. Promise." He throws me an apologetic smile before turning right at the intersection. "So what's wrong with Josh? Is he okay?"

I nod. I think he is okay. "He's fine. If I tell you what happened, would you promise not to laugh or tell Gabby or anyone else? I don't want Gabby to know because I know what she would say."

Lake promises not to tell, and I only hope he stays true to his word. I tell him what happened and he curses at the news.

"Is this the first time he has attempted suicide?" Lake wants to know.

"Yes, this is the first time he has tried to."

As I say this, I can't help but wonder what was going through Josh's head. I try to think of signs too that could have led to him wanting to do this to himself, but I couldn't think of anything. He seemed alright when I saw him earlier and even at school he seemed fine. I was aware of his condition, how someone with schizophrenia had a high suicide rate. Doctors had advised Lynn and Phillip to always keep an eye on him for any changes in his behaviour. There were days I knew Josh felt down, not just thinking about his parents' deaths, but the illness too. Bullying at school doesn't help when kids say he is crazy, which only makes him hate himself more. Or at least what society considers 'normal' when he was able to block out the voices and hallucinations, and you wouldn't expect that he had an illness. He always enjoyed my company, and always shared with me with what could be bothering him.

Yet, this was something he couldn't talk to me about.

Lake slows down at a red light, flicking on his blinker to turn right at the intersection. On the other side of the intersection, I see the blue sign with an arrow pointing to the right, and the hospital symbol. A wave of relief washed over me knowing that we were almost there.

"I want to apologise for this morning," Lake says, turning right once the light turns to green. "You know when you asked Gabby why Josh couldn't come to her party, and she just laughed at you while I smirked? Well, I feel bad for doing it. I wanted to tell her to be nicer, but she would give me a hard time for not following her."

"You have the right to stand up in what you believe, Lake," I say. "You shouldn't let Gabby control your thinking."

"I know I shouldn't."

The hospital comes into view and Lake pulls in, parking at the entrance.

"Thank you for the ride," I say as I unbuckle my seat belt.

"No problem. Do you need a ride back home? I can stay and wait for you."

I shake my head. Right now all I wanted was to be alone with Josh. "No, it's okay. There's no reason for you to hang around. Besides, Gabby will want you back at her party. One of Josh's parents will take me home later. Listen, I don't have a lot of cash on me at the moment, but I will give you money for petrol at school tomorrow."

Lake holds up his hand and shakes his head. "There's no need for you to pay me, Emily. I'm the one who offered, so don't worry about it."

I smile. "Okay. Thanks for the ride. I will see you in school tomorrow." I open the car door and get out.

"Emily?" Lake calls me just as I'm about to close the door.

"Yeah?"

"You're a loyal friend. You stick up for Josh, and you're always there when he needs you, especially with this illness he has. I don't think many people would do the things you do."

I stand there for a moment, taking in what he said. No one had said that to me before, and I was really surprised to hear it from Lake.

"Thanks, Lake."

I close the door and watch Lake drive away. I stand there for a moment, even after his car had disappeared, thinking about what he had said. I guess I am a loyal friend. I know I can easily choose to walk away and not be friends with him, not wanting to be apart of his life as he deals with his mental illness. But I have chosen to stay because he is my best friend. I would have wanted him to be there for me too if I was the one dealing with this illness. We have been there for each other for so long. Why would I walk away from this now?

I enter inside. The hospital was quiet and calm, and it seemed to be a slow night. There was no receptionist at the front desk, so I texted Lynn to let her know I was here, hoping the reception will be good in here and she would get my message. Thankfully it did go through, and she told me she will meet me.

I take a seat in the lobby. It wasn't long before Lynn enters. She looked like a total mess when I see her, her eyes red and puffy. I stand up from the couch.

"Emily, thank you for coming." She strolls over to me and wraps me into a hug.

"How is Josh?" I ask.

Lynn pulls away. "He is resting at the moment. He doesn't want Phil or me in the room right now. He said he wants to be alone, but I know he will be happy once he sees you."

"Are you and Phillip okay?"

She nods and gives me a small smile. She pats my shoulder. "We are okay. Just a little shaken up from what happened."

Lynn leads me down a few corridors until we get to the

ward Josh was staying in. Phillip is waiting outside of his room. I greet Phillip and then enter Josh's room.

Josh has the room to himself. He's asleep. There are straps on his wrists, legs and one across his waist to stop him from hurting himself. Quietly, I sat down on the chair that's beside him. I almost didn't want to look at him, not sure how I was going to react. The last time I saw him in hospital was right after his psychotic break that led to him being diagnosed with schizophrenia.

Josh must have sense someone being in the room. He opens his eyes and turns in my direction. A smile spread across his face when he sees me.

"Emily."

I return the smile, getting up from the chair to stand beside him. "Hey. I came as soon as I heard."

Josh shakes his head, looking sad. "You didn't have to come, Em." He turns away from me. "I don't want you to see me like this."

There's a tap at the door. I look over to see Phil. He tells me that he and Lynn are going to go to the cafeteria. I nod, and they leave.

I turn back to Josh, putting my hand on his shoulder. "What happened Josh? Why did you do it?"

Josh shakes off my hand and looks at the floor instead of meeting my eyes.

"That voice in my head, the one that has all of this power over all of the other voices... He told me I wasn't good enough, that I was wasting my time being alive and I should just kill myself because no one wants me here. That I'm not the son Lynn and Phillip wanted when they adopted me. I'm also ruining your life and that you don't really want to be my friend because of my illness… That I should be dead just like my parents and no one will ever miss me…"

My heart rip to pieces hearing this. I couldn't imagine how crappy Josh must have felt having this voice say those things to him. It… It was heartbreaking, and I wish I could be inside Josh's head and be the voice to tell him to never listen to those thoughts, that *I'm* the voice he should hear. It was bad enough with the bullying in school and what others said about him. He didn't need some voice only he could hear to make it worse.

I put my hand on his cheek, wiping the tears that are falling. "Josh, listen to me. You are worth it. Lynn and Phillip are proud to have you as their son, even if you aren't their biological son. They love you. And you aren't ruining my life, Josh. You're my best friend and I love having you around."

Josh nods, but doesn't say anything.

I sit back down in the chair. I watch him for a long time, the silence growing between us. I wanted Josh to open up to me.

I soon ask the question I'm afraid to know.

"Do you want to die, Josh? Is that why you tried to take your life?"

Josh remains silent. He looks to his right before turning his gaze to his bed. I wonder if any of his hallucinations were in the room with him, or if he was trying to avoid eye contact with me.

I thought of going, that maybe Josh just wanted to be alone, and that hurt the most. I have been there for Josh through all of his ups and downs as he adjusted to a new life with his adopted parents after going from one foster family to another after his parents' deaths. And I was there with him when he was diagnosed with his illness. I had promised him I will be with him no matter what, but right now he didn't want me here.

I'm about to tell Josh that I'm going to go and I will hopefully be able to see him tomorrow when he is feeling better, when he speaks.

"No, I don't." He still avoids my gaze, staring down at his sheets. "But sometimes I miss my parents and wish I was with them. Though missing them is not the only thing I have been depressed about. I'm still coming to terms with my illness, and some days I just want to be normal where I don't have to wonder if the voices I hear are real, or if I'm seeing something that is real. I do whatever I can to distract myself from hearing the voices when they become demanding and the medications help too. But tonight I just… I felt down and I allowed myself to listen to the voice. I wish I didn't." Josh forces himself to look at me. "I don't want to end my life. I want to be a successful musician someday, and I want to be around you, Emily. You're my best friend. I don't know what I would do without you."

My stomach does a somersault when he mentioned the word 'best friend'. I'm proud to be his friend, but sometimes I wanted more. I could tell him right now how I felt about him, hoping he will return the same feelings. I know Josh cares about me, but I'm not sure in what way. Does he care for me as a friend or does he care for me as a lover? The only way to know was to tell him, only I'm not sure how I will be able to take the rejection if he doesn't return the feelings. And telling him how I felt right now probably wasn't a good idea. I don't want to make him feel more guilty for what he did.

I try to hold back the tears as I stare at him. I wanted to kiss him so bad, to show what he meant to me. I wanted to tell him that everything was okay and we will get through this illness together. I wanted to tell him not to be afraid. But I couldn't find the right words to tell him.

I get up and hug him. I let the tears run wild as I sob into Josh's shoulder. I wish I could feel his arms around me.

"Emily, what's wrong?" Josh asks. He struggles to move his arms, but of course he couldn't move them with his arms strapped down. "Why are you crying?"

I pull away from Josh, wiping my eyes. I rest a hand on his right arm. "I'm just glad that nothing serious has happen to you. I don't want to lose you, Josh. I care about you so much. You mean the world to me. When Lynn called me to say you had attempted suicide, it really scared me."

I see the guilt in Josh's eyes. "I'm sorry if I made you feel like this." He looks around the room before turning back to me. "I wish I could hug you right now, but I can't. But can you sit down on the bed and hold me until you have to go?"

I nod, giving Josh a small smile. There wasn't much room, but I lie on my side with him, putting an arm around him as I snuggle my head against his shoulder. We lie there in silence for a while.

"Josh, can you please promise me something?" I say, breaking the silence.

"Like what?"

"I know it will be hard for you to promise, but can you please promise me that you won't do another suicide attempt? I really don't want to lose you."

He doesn't answer me straight away. "I promise, Emily. I'd do anything for you."

He kisses my forehead, and then snuggles his head against mine.

I want to believe the words he was saying, but it's hard to accept it. I'm scared the promise will be broken. Josh is good at keeping promises, yet this one I wasn't sure if he would keep.

* * *

Josh soon falls asleep. Carefully I get off the bed and sit back in the chair, texting Haylie to see how she was and to let her know how Josh was. I watch Josh sleep peacefully, but I knew I couldn't stay with him all night. I had school tomorrow. Phillip and Lynn drive me home.

"Thank you again for coming by, Emily," Lynn says as we get out of the car once it's parked in their driveway. "I know it meant a lot to Josh that you came tonight."

"It's no problem, Lynn. I'm just glad that Josh is alright."

Lynn smiles. "I'm glad too. I don't know what I would do if Phillip hadn't found him in time."

I turn to face Phillip. "Thank you, Phillip, for saving Josh."

He returns the smile. "It's alright, Emily."

"I'm sorry about pulling you out at that party earlier," Lynn apologises.

"Don't apologise. The party was lame anyway. Well, goodnight, Lynn, Phil. I will see you tomorrow."

They say goodnight in return. Lynn gives me a hug before she went inside with her husband. I headed back to mine. My parents were in the lounge room, waiting for me. It was way past my curfew, but they weren't going to get mad at me as Lynn called to let them know what was going on. They give me a hug and kiss, asking me how Josh was before telling me to head up to my room and to get ready for bed.

I lie in the darkness for a long time, staring at the outline of the poster on the back of my door of the grey kitten hanging from a branch, HANG IN THERE printed underneath the kitten. There was no way I was sleeping tonight. Not with Josh on my mind. I wonder if he too was lying awake in his room, and if he was upset that I wasn't there with him. I didn't want to think about what had happened, but it made me wonder what would happen if I hadn't gone to the party with Hailey. Would things have been different tonight if Josh and I had hung out? Would he had tried to take his own life?

Chapter 6

The hardest thing to do the next morning was to get out of bed. I didn't even feel like going to school at all. If I didn't have school, then I would have gone to the hospital to see Josh. Lynn and Phil had discussed with me on the way home that Josh will be transferred to a facility where he would be able to get help with his schizophrenia. It was the first time they were sending him to a place like this where he could get the proper help since he was diagnosed with the illness. The Hopkins wanted to do what they could do to help him, but with Josh being on suicide watch right now, they had discussed with a doctor that leaving him in hospital would be best for him. I know Josh is not going to agree with it, as he always feared that he will be taken away or that his adopted parents no longer wanted him. But this was for the best right now until Josh could get better. It has been discussed once that putting him into hospital would be a better option for him to get the help he needed, but it was decided that the best place for him was at home where he could be with his family. This time though it will be different. Doctors will be monitoring his medication and he would be asked to join in group sessions and activities, helping him on ways to improve his mental health.

Haylie waits for me at the front of the school. I kiss my mother goodbye and she hands me a twenty dollar note for lunch. I thank her, even though right now I just didn't care for food. Not with Josh on my mind. I barely had an appetite for breakfast this morning, but I didn't want my parents to worry so I ate a slice of toast.

"Have you heard anything from him this morning?"

Haylie asks me once Mum drove away.

I shake my head. "No, I haven't heard anything from him this morning. I will probably find out later how he is. He is going to be taken to a mental health facility to get some help."

"That's good. I'm glad he is alright, and that he is getting the help he needs."

"Same here. Josh really scared me last night, and I'm thankful he was saved in time."

Hailey touches my shoulder. "I'm glad too."

We sit under our favourite tree. I can't help but feel a sinking sad feeling in my heart, looking at the empty seat to my right where Josh would be right now if he was here.

"So, what's happening to your car?" I ask Haylie, switching the subject so we weren't talking about Josh.

Haylie shrugs. "I don't know. My dad is taking it to the mechanic this morning. He said he will help me pay the repairs if it costs me too much. You know what? I should get Elliot and Ron to pay for the damage. Why should my dad pay for it when they are the ones who vandalised it?"

"You know that's never going to happen. I mean, they will deny they even went near your car."

Hailey agrees. "You're right."

I take out my diary with my timetable to check what my first class was this morning. I groan when I see that it's maths. I'm in no mood to learn about numbers. I hate numbers. I really do. I wish maths didn't even exist.

When the bell rings for first period, Haylie and I head to class together. We're the first ones to reach the classroom. I glance over at where Josh would be sitting right now as I walk over to my desk, a wave of sadness washing over me. I kept my eyes on his desk as I sit down next to Haylie. It just feels weird without him being here.

"So Freak attempted suicide." I glance up and see Gabby walking over to us with her friend Samantha alongside her. Lake trails behind them. Gabby laughs. "And let me guess, it wasn't successful? What a pathetic loser he is."

My heart crushes at her comment. How could she say something like that? And how did she know what Josh…

Lake. Lake broke his promise of not saying anything and told the heartless bitch.

"Gabby, I told you not to say that," Lake says.

"Shut up, Lake," Gabby replies. "I'm doing the talking and I will say whatever I please."

I glance at Lake, hurt that he would betray me. "You told her, Lake? After I told you not to tell her what happened to Josh?"

Lake looks at me guilty. "I'm sorry, Emily. I didn't want to tell her. She forced it out of me."

Gabby smirks. "It's true. I did. I can't believe how pathetic Freak is."

I narrow my eyes at her.

"Gabby, don't you have something better to do than insult people just because you think you're better than them?" Haylie asks. "Because trust me, you aren't better than others."

Gabby ignores her, putting all of her attention on me. Other students were starting to enter the classroom. I really hope Mr Carlson comes in soon. I really don't feel comfortable with Gabby and her friends standing here, saying nasty stuff about Josh. I wonder how Gabby can even live with herself for the heartless things she says about people.

"So, why did Freak attempt suicide?" Gabby went on to harass me. "Doesn't he like his life?"

I continue to ignore her. She wasn't worth fighting with. I open my bag to pull out my equipment I needed for the lesson.

Gabby snatches my bag from me. "Hey, I'm talking to you!" She tips my bag upside down, and all of my books and pencil case fell out. Some books landed on my desk while the others landed on the floor, along with my pencil case. I feel my classmates' eyes on me.

Samantha bends down to pick up something from the floor.

"Gabby, this is totally unnecessary," Lake says.

"So, are you going to answer the question?" Gabby leans on my desk, putting her face directly up to mine.

"Why would I want to tell you what goes on with Josh when this is the way you treat him and call him names?" I answer, narrowing my eyes at her.

"Well, you told my boyfriend. So, you can tell me."

"Hey, Gabby, take a look at this," Samantha says as she gets up from the floor. She hands Gabby my maths book.

My body freezes when I see the back of the book open, full of the doodles I made during class.

"What is it, Samantha?" Gabby takes the book.

My stomach began to tie into knots. My secret crush on Josh was about to be reveal to my entire class. I was going to be laugh at. I know what everyone is going to think about me liking Josh. No. This can't be happening.

I should have fake being sick so I didn't have to go to school today, and visited Josh at the hospital instead. It would have saved the humiliation.

"Aw." Gabby looks at me. "You love Josh." She turns to the class, holding up the book in the air to show everyone my doodles. "Hey everyone, Emily Carter is in love with Freak."

Some students snicker at this, others just went on to mind their own business. I don't know why it was so wrong for me to like him.

"Gabby, cut it out," Lake says. "This is starting to get out of hand."

Gabby closes the book and set it down on my desk. "So does Freak know you like him? Oh, wait. I bet you haven't told him because you know he can't love you back. Do you want to know why he can't love you back?"

I stood up from my seat. I had enough of Gabby's nasty comments. How would she feel if people were to call her names because she had a mental illness?

I tense my jaw. "Don't ever speak like that way about Josh, you hear me, Gabby? Just because he has a mental illness, doesn't mean you can say this stuff about him. His illness doesn't define who he is. He is a normal person just like everyone else."

Gabby smirks. "Whatever."

I clench my fist and punch Gabby in her jaw. The classroom

is silence, shock by my actions.

Gabby puts a hand over her jaw. "Ow, you bitch!"

"Emily Carter." I glance over to where Mr Carlson had just walked into the classroom, witnessing my punch. "Go to the principal's office this instant."

I sigh. Of course I'm the one to be in trouble, not Gabby.

I avoid looking at anyone as I pick up my stuff and placing it in my bag. Going to see Mr Mathison in his office was the last thing I wanted, and I wasn't known to be in trouble. I have never been sent to the principal's office before. But at least going to the principal's office was better than sitting in a subject I don't even like, and listening to Gabby say awful things about Josh.

And now my secret has been exposed, how was Gabby going to use that information?

My teacher quickly writes a note to the principal and made me leave the room. I walk out of the classroom as fast as I could, afraid to meet Gabby's gaze, who I know will have a smirk on her face. Once in the hall, I burst into tears. I cry a little before quickly wiping them and walk to the principal's office. I didn't want Mr Mathison to see I had been crying.

I sit outside his office until he calls me in. I sit down in front of his desk, a million things wandering through my mind on what kind of punishment Mr Mathison was going to give me. I only hoped he wasn't going to call my parents. And I knew Gabby wasn't going to be in trouble for the nasty things she had said.

I hand over the note that Mr Carlson had written. Mr Mathison reads the note.

He looks up at me, surprise. "You punched Gabrielle Casey?"

"She deserves it."

Mr Mathison put the note down on his desk. "No one deserves to be hit, Emily."

"Well, Gabby does. I'm so tired of her making fun of Josh and getting away with it."

Mr Mathison folds his arms across his desk. "Emily, do I need to remind you what the school rules are about violence?"

I shake my head, answering no.

"Listen, Emily. You're an excellent student, and I would hate to give you detention or suspend you. I know you don't like anyone making fun of Josh, but if you ever have a problem with someone, I do not want you to take matters in your own hands. I want you to come see me, and I will deal with it."

I wanted to laugh at this. I really did. I doubt whatever he was telling me was true. Even if Mr Mathison did talk to Gabby about her disrespectful behaviour towards Josh, she wouldn't listen to him. She will act all innocent, promising she will be kind to him. And once she leaves the principal's office, she will go back to being her normal disrespectful self. Besides, Gabby gets away with everything. She wouldn't even get punished for bullying Josh.

"Gabby will continue doing it even if you did tell her to stop bullying Josh," I tell him. "That's why I punched her because I just couldn't take it anymore. She's a horrible person."

"Again, there is no reason for you to use violence. Now, I'm going to let you off with a warning. The next time you use any form of violence, I will either give you detention or I will suspend you. I will also contact your parents."

"And what about Gabby? Are you going to be punishing her too for bullying Josh? Do you realise that she does this every day? Not just her, but others too. Yesterday morning Ron Gold and Elliot Cox tried to stir up trouble for him, but Hailey

Connors and I stopped them."

"If I see them do anything, I will be speaking to them."

"Bull crap."

Mr Mathison gives me a disapproving look. "Do you want to be issued with a detention, Miss Carter?"

I shake my head.

"Then I suggest you don't use that language or speak that way to me. Now, I will let you go back to class, and I do not want to see you in my office again."

I didn't talk back at him this time, even if I wanted to say what I really think. But I couldn't risk getting detention or being suspended. My parents will kill me for being suspended.

Mr Mathison dismisses me. I took my time walking back to class.

Chapter 7

"Hey, Emily." I spin around at the sound of my name as I exit the building once school ended for the day. I see Lake hurrying over to catch up to me. "Can I talk to you?"

I wanted to tell him to go away and leave me alone. After what happened between me and Gabby this morning, I didn't really want to associate with anyone who were friends with her. I especially didn't want to talk to Lake, not after he betrayed me with telling his girlfriend what had happened with Josh after he'd promised me he wouldn't say anything. But I decided not to be rude and hear what Lake has to say.

"What about?" I ask him once he reaches me.

Lake grabs my arm and pulls me aside from the crowd of students. We stand around the corner of the building. He looks around, where I was sure he was probably looking out for Gabby, the fear in his eyes showed that he was worried about being caught being seen with me.

He turns to me. "Sorry. I don't want Gabby to see me talking to you. Look, I need you to listen to me. I know you're mad at me because I told Gabby about Josh. I'm sorry. I really am, Emily. I was going to keep my promise, but when I got back to her place, she was mad at me. She wanted to know where I had gone to. I told her I was helping out someone, and then she wanted to know what I was helping you out with. She forced it out of me and I told her. I'm sorry, Emily. Please forgive me."

I stare at Lake, his brown eyes begging me to forgive him. He was telling the truth. I truly do feel sorry for him. I would so hate to have someone like Gabby as my boyfriend.

"It's okay, Lake," I tell him. "Since you apologise and you were trying your best earlier to stop Gabby from saying those things to me, I forgive you."

He smiles at me, showing off his white teeth. "Thanks, Emily. I want you to know that if you need someone to talk to about Josh, I'm here for you."

I stare at him, unsure why he was being so kind to me. He is never this kind to me. I couldn't help but wonder if he was up to something. I mean, why would he all of a sudden want to talk to me about Josh? He has never given a damn about him. He stays clear of him, like Josh would turn into some kind of monster that everyone makes him out to be just because he has schizophrenia. He also follows Gabby's footsteps of making fun of him.

"Since when do you want to talk about Josh?" I ask him. "No one ever wants to talk about him. And if they do, it's only to talk nasty about him."

"I promise I won't talk nasty about him. I just thought that if something is bothering you, I could be the one you would like to talk to."

I still wasn't sure if Lake was someone I could trust. "I will see."

"So, is it true? Do you actually have a crush on him?"

"Yes. Why?"

"Nothing. I'm just surprise, that's all. I mean, I have always thought you're just friends."

There's a pinch in my heart as he mentions this. "We are friends."

"Does Josh know you like him more than a friend?"

I shake my head. "No. I've never told him what my feelings are for him. I'm scared to tell him just in case it affects our friendship or he doesn't see me more than that." And right now I really didn't want to be talking about this with Lake. He doesn't need to know anything about Josh and I. "Listen, can we talk about this some other time? I really need to go."

I push pass Lake, heading towards the entrance of the school where I hope my Mum will be waiting for me.

I'd only taken a few steps when he calls out to me. "Emily?"

I turn back to him. "Yeah?"

"Can I make it up to you for telling Gabby about Josh by taking you out to dinner?"

I stand there, my mouth hanging slightly open. I didn't know what to think when he asked me that. Lake Terra isn't hitting on me, is he?

Crap. That's the last thing I need him to do. What will Gabby think?

"Like in a date?" Lake nods. "Lake, you're with Gabby. She will be pissed with you for taking me out. Even if we go as friends, she would still be pissed." And I don't want to know what she will do with me if she finds out we went out together.

I'm already Gabby's enemy. Going out with Lake will make it worse. And she will never care if I'm not interested in him; she would think I'm trying to steal him when I'm not.

And what would Josh say if I was to go out with him? What if Josh felt something towards me?

"Forget about Gabby. I'm breaking up with her tonight. After those things she said about Josh and to you, I can't stand to be with her anymore. And I'm really glad you punched her. She deserved it." He smiles.

I return the smile. "Well, I'm glad that someone appreciates me punching her."

"So, would you like to go out with me?"

I stand there, staring at him. I still don't understand why all of a sudden Lake was being so nice to me. Even if I did agree to go out with him, my heart is set on Josh. How am I supposed to tell Lake that without hurting his feelings?

"I have a lot of things on my mind right now, Lake," I say. "Maybe I will consider it, but only as friends."

Lake smiles. "Okay, Em."

Without saying anything else, I turn away, heading towards the street where I saw Mum waiting for me. I greet Mum and hop into the car.

* * *

Mum drives me to the mental health facility to see Josh. She comes in with me. We find Josh in the common room, where he is sitting in a chair beside a large window, glancing outside. There's a tree there with two rainbow lorikeets sitting on the branch, and Josh watches them quietly.

"Hey, Josh," I say as Mum and I stood beside him.

Josh turns his attention away from the tree and turns to me. He smiles, getting up from his seat and hugs me. He looks like a mess, like he hadn't gotten much sleep and his hair was a total mess. He is dressed in a grey tracksuit and blue shirt that his parents must have brought in for him.

"It's good to see you, Emily."

"How have you been, Josh?" Mum asks him.

Josh pulls away from me and looks at Mum. "I'm good, thanks Carrie."

Mum smiles. "I'm glad to hear that." She turns to me, putting a hand on my back. "I will leave you two so you can be alone. I will wait outside."

I nod. "You know you can stay, Mum."

"Yeah, you can stay. I don't mind," Josh tells her.

Mum smiles at us. "I know. I just feel you two would like to be alone and talk. I'm glad you're doing well, Josh. I hope the treatments here will help you."

Josh gives her a smile. "Thanks, Carrie. I hope so too."

Mum leaves us. Josh gestures to a lounge, and we sit down. "Are you doing okay in here?" I ask him.

His eyes don't meet mine as he nods, glancing around the room. "Yeah. It's kind of boring in here though." He turns his attention back to me. "I mean, there are activities I can do if I don't want to stay in my room. The staff here watches you like a hawk, making sure you take your medication. It makes me nervous a little having someone watching me. I keep thinking something bad will happen with everyone watching me."

I rest a hand on Josh's and give him a small smile. "Everything will be fine. Just stick to your treatments and you will be out of here in no time. Did the doctor say when you could leave?"

Josh shakes his head. "No, he hasn't."

"Did Lynn and Phillip come see you today?"

He nods. "Yeah, they came early this morning to see how I was doing before they went off to work. I'm so happy you are here, Emily. I was worried you weren't going to come."

I squeeze Josh's hand. "Josh, you know I'm going to come see you no matter what. Although tomorrow I won't be coming to visit because I have my driving test. But I will definitely come visit on Saturday. I probably be able to stay longer as visiting hours are almost up. But I'm glad I'm able to come visit this afternoon. I have been thinking about you all day."

"Same here, Em. I have missed you. Oh, and all the best for your test tomorrow. You're going to do great."

"Thanks. Maybe when you get out of here, I will take you for a spin in the car."

He smiles brightly. "I would love that. So, anything interesting happened at school today?"

I don't look at Josh as I replay back the things that had happened today. I really didn't want to be reminded of the things Gabby had said or how I almost gotten detention, maybe even suspended if it had been serious, for punching her. And of course, I didn't want to be reminded of Lake. I'm still trying to process what he had asked me this afternoon.

I turn back to him. "School is the same thing like always. And Gabby is always up to no good."

Josh looks at me concern, like he could see that I wasn't fully telling him the truth about everything that happened at school today.

"What did Gabby do, Em? Did she hurt you?"

I shake my head. "No. It's more like I hurt her. She was saying stuff I didn't like, and I just punched her in the jaw for it. Of course, Mr Carlson walked in at the time I did it, and not at the time when Gabby said the things she said."

Josh squeezes my hand. "I'm glad you are okay. And I'm glad that someone finally punched her. I just never thought it would be you to do it."

I laugh. "Yeah, I'm still quite surprise myself. I'm thankful that Mr Mathison let me off on a warning. I was so sure he was going to give me a detention or worse, suspend me."

"Well, I'm glad he didn't suspend you. I don't know what I would do without you at school."

I smile and then rest my head on his shoulder. Josh wraps his arms around me.

"I hope you get to leave soon," I say.

"Same here. I have only been here for a day, and I already feel like I'm losing my mind. The doctor was saying to Lynn and Phil that if I do all of my treatments, talk with a psychologist each day and take part in activities, then maybe I only have to stay here for a week. But still the doctor can't guarantee how long I will be here."

"Let's hope it's for a week." I pull away from him. "I also collected your homework. I don't know if you will be able to do it in here, but I will give it to Lynn. They should let you do it while you're in here. At least it gives you something to do rather than staring out the window."

Josh laughs. "Yeah, I guess so. I can't wait to get home so I can play my guitar."

"You will be home soon. I will come over and you can play me something."

Josh smiles. "I will definitely keep that in mind."

Chapter 8

I wished I could have stayed with Josh a little longer, but visiting hours ended at five o'clock. I told Josh that I will come by on Saturday as I will be doing my driving test tomorrow afternoon. I only hope that I will do well with it and not let Josh occupy my mind.

I lie wide awake later that night, thinking about Josh and wondering how he was, and what he was doing. I wonder if he too was lying awake thinking about me.

I do my best to get what sleep I could, because the last thing I wanted was to do my driving test half asleep. By the morning, all I wanted to do was stay under the covers and not even care about attending school. I especially didn't want to see Gabby after yesterday, but what choice did I have? I had to face her eventually.

Mum lets me drive to school that morning, making sure

I get as much last-minute practice in for the test. Dad was picking me up after school today to take me to do my test.

I pull up to the kerb at the front of the school, shifting the gear into park and apply the handbrake before switching off the engine.

Mum takes out my logbook from the glove box and began signing it. "You did excellent, Emily. You are going to do well this afternoon. I have faith you will pass."

I smile brightly. "Thanks. I just hope I won't be too tired later."

Mum looks up from the logbook. "You didn't get a lot of sleep last night?"

I shake my head, unbuckling my seat belt. "I had trouble sleeping last night."

"Was it because you were nervous about the test?"

I shake my head. "Just thinking about Josh, and hoping he will be okay."

Mum reaches over and pats my shoulder. "He is going to be fine, Emily. Joshua is in a good place right now and getting the help he needs to get better. He will be home soon."

I nod. "I know. It just feels hard without him being here."

"I know, sweetie. But I promise you that everything will end up being fine."

I say goodbye to Mum and step out of the car, grabbing my bag from the back seat. Mum finishes signing the logbook before getting into the driver's seat and pulls away from the kerb.

Haylie hurries over to me.

"Emily, you will never guess what I had just heard," she says. "Everyone is talking about it."

"What is it?" I ask her.

"Lake broke up with Gabby last night."

I was surprise to hear this. Okay, I knew about it because Lake told me he was going to do it, but I wasn't expecting him to act on it.

I mention this to Haylie.

"I never expected he would break up with her," Haylie continues on. "I would have expected him to forget all about it because no doubt Gabby would have bribe him with something to stay with her."

I nod in agreement. "Of course. But it seems like Lake didn't give in to it."

"So, did you get to see Josh yesterday?"

We start making our way to the tree to wait for the bell to ring. "I did."

"How is he doing?"

"He is doing well. He is responding to the treatment. He may be able to leave after a week if he keeps doing well."

"That's good. I might see if I can stop by to see him over the weekend."

"I'm going tomorrow if you would like to come with me. I'm sure Josh will like your company."

"He will. So, your driving test is this afternoon. Nervous?"

"Very." I sit down on the seat under the tree. Haylie sits down beside me.

"You're going to do well with it, Emily."

"Thanks."

I knew I would, and all I could think about when I get my licence is hoping to go somewhere with Josh where it can just be the two of us.

* * *

Dad drives me over to Hailey's after I had done the test. It was last minute, something we had discussed at school, but we had asked our parents if Hailey could spend the night at my place. We both thought it would be easier if she did, when we left in the morning to see Josh.

While Dad stays in the car, I headed up the lawn of Hailey's house and ring the doorbell. Inside I can hear the television on full blast with explosions and gun shots. No one came to answer for a few minutes. I wasn't sure if anyone had heard me over the noise, so I ring the doorbell the second time.

"Coming!" Hailey's elder brother Elijah, by two years, calls from the other side.

I hear his footsteps before the door swings open. Elijah, who was almost the splitting image of his sister with short blonde hair and blue eyes and the same square jawline as her, answers the door, a Coke can in his hand.

"Emily, hey!" He gestures me in. "Come on in."

I step over the threshold and stand aside in the hallway as Elijah closes the door. I peek into the lounge room to see Elijah's four friends in there. Two of them sat in front of the television, cursing and hitting the buttons on the controller fast as they play some shooting game with zombies, while the other two yell out things about the game.

Elijah gestures towards the lounge room. "Sorry about the noise. We thought we would play a game before band practice later."

I give him a smile. "It's fine. Don't worry about it. I won't be here for long anyway."

"Right. My sister is spending the night at yours." He nods towards the kitchen next to the lounge room. "Come wait in the kitchen."

He moves first and I follow him, passing the bathroom where I heard the shower running.

We enter the kitchen. Elijah makes a beeline to the fridge.

"Do you want something to drink while you're waiting?" he asks, opening the fridge before I even reply with an answer. "Haylie told me she shouldn't take too long. She is taking a quick shower. To be honest, she has been in there for like half an hour." He shakes his head and I laugh, standing at the kitchen counter. "I don't know why she is taking forever." He looks in the fridge. "What would you like? Water, Coke, Sprite?"

"I will have a Sprite, thanks."

He grabs the can, kicking the fridge door shut, and hands me the can. It's cold in my hand as I open it, taking a sip.

"How come you're home today?" I ask. "Don't you have work?"

He shakes his head. "Day off." He sips his drink.

"Good for you."

"How's Josh? Haylie told me what happened."

I nod slowly, not looking at him as I tap my finger tips on the can. "He's okay. I saw him yesterday." I force myself to meet Elijah's eyes. "He isn't himself, but I hope being in the hospital he will get the help he needs to get better."

Elijah gives me an assuring smile. "He will, Emily. He will get through this with the right help."

I smile, nodding. Elijah was right. Josh was going to get through this with the right help. He had so many up and downs since he was diagnosed with his illness. He got through it as he adjusted to his new lifestyle, and I'm sure he will get through this too.

"You're right, Elijah."

Yelling comes from the lounge room for a brief second, and then Elijah's friends quieten down again as they go back to their game. Elijah holds up his finger to tell me to hold on a second, and leaves the kitchen.

While he is gone, I send a quick text to Dad to tell him Haylie is still getting ready, and we will be out soon. As I'm putting the phone back in the skirt pocket of my school uniform that I haven't changed out of yet, I hear Elijah talking to Haylie before he emerges into the kitchen.

"Haylie said she will be out in a minute." He nods towards the direction of the lounge room. "I also told the guys to quieten down. Once you girls leave, we might start practice. Our parents should be home soon." He drinks, walking over to me.

"How is your band going?"

"It's going great." He stands next to me. "We are waiting to hear back on a gig."

I smile. "That is great."

"It is. When we do get it, be sure to come see us. Josh is welcome to come too."

"I wouldn't miss it for the world."

I have heard him play his music a few times when I have been over here. He started his band Breaking Summer last year, punk pop being their main genre. Their music is really good and I hope the band goes far.

Elijah smiles, drinking the last of his drink and sets it on the counter.

"So, what are you two up to tonight?" he wants to know, leaning back on the counter.

I shrug. "We haven't decided yet, but we will most likely sit back for the evening watching a movie."

Footsteps are heard behind us, and Haylie comes bouncing in the room with a grin.

"Did you get it?" she asks.

I innocently smile, shaking my head. "I'm going to reveal if I pass tomorrow when we see Josh. I want to tell you guys together."

Haylie groans. "Oh, come on, Emily. Don't let me wait until tomorrow. Tell me now, please."

I chuckle. "All will be revealed tomorrow."

"What's this?" Elijah asks, darting his eyes between us, completely left out of the conversation.

"I went for my licence today."

"Well, if you aren't going to tell my sister how you went, maybe you can tell me once she leaves the room."

Haylie slaps her brother's arm playfully. "I'm not leaving the room."

"Okay!" Elijah holds up his arms in surrender to avoid another slap from his sister. "Well, after Emily reveals the results tomorrow, remember to tell me too." He pats my arm gently. "But in case my sister doesn't mention anything tomorrow, congratulations if you pass. If you didn't, you will do well next time."

I smile. "Thanks, Elijah." I turn to Haylie. "Come on, let's go. My Dad is waiting outside."

We turn to leave, saying goodbye to Elijah.

As we walk out of the kitchen, Elijah calls out, "Say hi to Josh for me."

"We will," we call out together.

* * *

The next day I went to see Josh with Haylie, beaming from the happiness yesterday. Josh is in his room when we arrived. He was about to head out to the common room, and suggest to us we could hang out there. But before we head there, I just had to tell him the good news I have been dying to tell him and Haylie since yesterday afternoon.

Making sure none of the nurses were looking or that the security cameras were pointing in my direction, I pull out my paper licence that I had to hold onto until I receive my actual licence in ten days from my pocket. I had to sneak this in as all of my belongings had to be kept outside in a locker.

"I passed!" I blurt out, waving the paper licence.

Josh smiles, taking the paper in his hands. "Emily, that's great!" He wraps me into a hug. "I'm so happy for you."

I return the smile as I pull away from him. I take the paper from him, and quickly folded it up, placing it back into my pocket before any nurses see it.

Haylie high-fives me, relieved I finally announced the news that I had been keeping from her. She hugs Josh next. "It's good to see you are doing well, Josh. Emily has been keeping me updated on how you're doing."

"Well, there isn't really much to do here. I can't wait to get out of here and go home."

We make our way to the common room.

"Lynn and Phillip are coming later," Josh tells us. "We plan to have lunch together."

"That's nice," I say. "My parents plan to stop by tomorrow to see how you're doing."

"They don't need to do that."

"I know, but they wanted to."

"Well, I look forward to their visit tomorrow."

We sit down on the couch in the common room, catching up with Josh on what has been happening for the past few days at school. The butterflies dance around my stomach as the three of us talk and laugh. I like being this close to Josh, and I like him being happy. I couldn't wait for him to come home.

Chapter 9

I visited Josh each day. My parents came to visit Sunday like they said they will and we sat down to have lunch with him. After school I stay with him until visiting hours were over, talking to him about school, and things we could do once he got out of the hospital. I was hoping to bring his homework so we could work on it together, but nothing from the outside was allowed to be brought inside where Josh or other patients could potentially harm themselves. Although I honestly didn't see the harm in bringing our books to do homework. It wasn't like Josh would harm himself with the books.

At school, Gabby still made her smart-ass comments about Josh. I had to do everything I could to resist doing something I would regret. Clearly I didn't punch her hard enough. On Monday she asked me how he was doing and how long will he be in the psych ward, saying it's where he belongs. She even asked if he was put in a straitjacket. I ignore everything she had said. She obviously didn't know what she was talking about.

Wednesday afternoon Josh decided he wanted to do something different rather than hanging out in the common room. There's a courtyard that we could go out to and enjoy the sun. It's freezing outside, and we do our very best to ignore the cold.

"So I had a meeting with my parents and the doctor this morning," Josh tells me as we sit down on a stone bench.

"Oh yeah? What was it about?"

"He said that I will be able to come home on Friday." Josh smiles. "I'm coming home, Emily."

I smile, wrapping him into a hug. "That's great, Josh."

"He said I have been doing well to treatment here and taking part in group sessions that he said I can come home."

"I'm very happy, Josh. So now that you're being release, how do you feel since you were admitted?"

"Besides going completely out of my mind from boredom? I feel better. I have been trying my hardest to block out the voices, especially the one that was really demanding about me taking my life. The same with the hallucinations, I have been trying to block them out too. Georgia though has been hanging around, keeping me company. It's hard to ignore her without hoping anyone notices. Aspen visited too, talking to me about his washed-up rock star life. I really don't like Aspen. He complains too much and really sucks out the energy."

I put my hand on his shoulder. "I'm glad that everything is working out well."

"Same. The hardest thing is not letting the delusion that people here might harm me get to me. I know everyone is doing what they can do to help me get better." He takes a deep breath and then exhales it slowly. "It's so frustrating juggling with all of this. Some days I feel like I'm not going to be able to cope. Sometimes I wish my parents were here, because I know they will be able to get me through it." He turns to look away, staring at the ground.

I take Josh's hand and squeeze it. "Josh, look at me."

He looks up at me.

"Don't be so harsh on yourself, okay?" Josh nods. "I know the last eleven years has been hard on you losing your parents. And I wish they were here right now too. I would love to meet them. Lynn and Phillip may not be your biological parents, but they love you and they do everything they can to help you to get the treatment you need. What you are going through is hard, but you're doing well. You will get through this, Josh. And I'll always be here to support you."

Josh smiles. "Thank you, Emily. I'm thankful to have you as a friend."

There's a pinch in my heart again at the mention of the word 'friend'. It was clear that's what he saw me as, and I would never be more than that to him. But even if we couldn't be more than friends, I still loved him and I knew we were going to be friends for life. I couldn't imagine my life without him.

* * *

Friday came fast, and all I wanted was for school to be over so I could go home and see Josh. We plan to spend the night together, maybe watch a movie and to also listen to Josh play the guitar.

"I will come over tomorrow," Haylie says as we walk through the crowded corridor at the end of the day. "Maybe the three of us could go out for lunch or maybe see a movie."

I nod, smiling. "Josh will definitely like that after the week he has had."

"Hey, do you think Josh will be able to attend a music event?"

"I'm sure he will be able to once he gets out of the hospital." Although Lynn I'm sure will be watching him like a hawk, and who knew if she will allow him out of her sight for a few hours.

We walk outside the building.

"You know Elijah's band?"

"Of course I do."

"They got their first gig at a club next Thursday night. Elijah said to invite you and Josh along. Do you think he would want to come along?"

I squeal. "Oh my gosh! That's great! I will definitely be there. And of course Josh will come. He enjoys all kinds of music. Anything to distract him from the voices in his head."

Haylie stops walking, her face beaming. "Hey, I have an idea." She turns to me. "I will discuss it with Elijah though. Has Josh ever performed his music in front of an audience?"

I shake my head. "No, never. He has only ever played his music in front of me. He doesn't even perform in front of Mrs Hartley when he has an assignment to do for Music. He records his assignments for her."

"Why does he do that?"

I shrug. "I don't know. I think he is just shy of what others might say about his music."

"Do you think if I ask my brother to allow Josh to perform some songs, do you think he would do it?"

I shrug. Josh had talked about maybe becoming a musician someday, but I'm not sure if he will ever take that path, or if he would do it as a hobby. Maybe getting the opportunity to get up on stage and perform would help his shyness or maybe its stage fight he has, give him the confidence he needs to perform in front of others instead of me.

"I will talk with him and see what he will say," I answer. "I think he would really like that."

Haylie smiles brightly. "I know he will. Let me know what he says."

I nod. "I will."

"Emily!"

Haylie and I turn to see Lake hurrying over to catch up to us.

Haylie rolls her eyes. "What does he want now?"

Lake reaches us. "Hey, can I talk to you for a sec?"

I turn to Haylie. "I will call you later, okay?"

Haylie nods and we say our goodbyes before she wanders off. Her dad was picking her up this afternoon so they could go to pick up her car after it was at the mechanic for a week.

I turn my attention to Lake. "What can I do for you, Lake?"

"I just want to ask you how Josh is doing."

"Josh is doing well. In fact, he is coming home from the hospital today."

Lake smiles. "That's great to hear, Emily. So, he will be back at school next week?"

I nod. "He will be."

"I'm glad he is doing well. I guess I will see him on Monday then. Have a nice weekend, Emily."

"You too, Lake."

Lake walks off and I follow behind him. I see Mum's car parked out front, and headed over.

She smiles at me as I got into the car. "Hey, sweetie. How

was your day?"

"It was good." I put on my seat belt. "The day seemed to go slow. All I wanted was to get home and see Josh."

"Well, you will be able to see him soon." Mum turns the ignition. "But first I need to get some things at the shops before we go home."

"No problems, Mum."

* * *

I don't see Josh until later that night. After completing my homework, I climb across the tree and climb through his bedroom window. He embraces me as soon as I'm inside.

"I miss you so much, Em," he says, sweeping me off my feet and spins me around.

I laugh. "You saw me like almost every day since you were at the hospital."

He puts me down and pulls me away. "I know, but that wasn't the same. I miss being able to hang out with you and doing our own thing. We couldn't really do that at the hospital."

"True, we couldn't, but we can do that now." I sit down on the edge of his bed. "Tomorrow Haylie is coming over. She suggested we go out for lunch and maybe catch a movie."

Josh joins me on the bed. "Awesome. I look forward to it."

He looks over at his guitar that's sitting near his desk, and gets up to grab it. Seeing the guitar made me remember what Haylie and I were discussing this afternoon.

"Hey, Josh, do you think you would ever perform in front of an audience?" I ask him.

Josh looks over at me as he picks up his guitar. "I don't know. I guess someday. At the moment I just feel paranoid with what people might think of what I'm playing. Like will they like it or would it be terrible? But my worse fear is what if I get a hallucination and something happens to ruin the performance."

I give him a warm smile. "I'm pretty sure none of that will happen, Josh."

He shrugs, coming back over to the bed. "It could." He sits down next to me with the guitar on his lap. "Why do you think I don't perform my music assignments in front of Mrs Hartley? I mean, she is a great teacher, but I just feared that I will freak out when she marks down my grade."

I put a hand on his shoulder to assure him that it would be okay. Although I was not in his class because I'm not musically gifted like Josh, I remember just before Josh was diagnosed with schizophrenia, he panicked right as he was meant to perform an assignment. He never had problems performing, he just never wanted to do it in front of a huge audience because he felt like he wasn't ready to do that. He always rejected the idea when any of the music teachers suggest he performs something for an assembly or a special event at school. I figured maybe it was just stage fright, but that wasn't the case at all. Even though playing music helped him to block out the voices in his head, Josh said that there is this one dominant voice that still finds a way to get to him and mess with his head. And that one day when he had to performed in front of the class and his teacher, as he started to play, the dominant voice stopped him, telling him no one will like his performance. He then got this delusional thought that everyone in the classroom was a spy, and that the music he was playing was going to get him into trouble by the government. He left the classroom before he blurted out anything that would make him seem like he was crazy. After Josh, Mrs Hartley and his parents sat down to discuss what had happened, Mrs Hartley was happy to allow Josh to film his performance if that made him comfortable. She also suggested that he could perform in front of her and not with the other students, but Josh still didn't feel comfortable.

After he was diagnosed, it became understood for how he had acted. Mrs Hartley never hassled Josh to perform in class again, even when he started taking his medication to help him with the paranoia and delusions, she continued to allow him to record is performance for her to mark. Many other students didn't like that. With music always calming him, she started allowing him to come to the classroom during lunch if he needed quiet time to play the guitar.

But I hope he will take Haylie's offer if her brother and his band allowed it. I'm pretty sure he will enjoy performing on the stage.

"You can say no to this if you want, but Haylie suggested something today," I say. "On Thursday she has invited us to go see her brother's band perform, and she said she can probably get him to allow you to perform a song or two on stage. How would you feel about that, Josh?"

Josh doesn't make eye contact with me straight away. He stares at the floor, his mind lost in his own thoughts.

"I don't know, Em. I mean, what if something happens on the stage?"

"Nothing will happen, Josh, because I will be there."

He looks up at me.

"You always said you would like to perform for an audience someday, and I know you don't want to because you fear something will happen. But I think this will be a great opportunity for you to get over that fear. And when you get up on the stage, keep your focus on me. Don't look at anyone besides me."

He smiles. "You know, if I agree to this, Aspen is going to be pissed at me."

I look around me, wondering if any of Josh's hallucinations were present with us right now.

"Let Aspen be pissed," I say. "He can be pissed all he wants because nothing he says matters because he isn't real. And if he does get upset, it's probably because he is jealous. He's a washed-up rock star who probably wasn't even any good so now he takes his negative vibe out on you."

Josh bursts into laughter at this. "You're right, Emily." He calms down. "Do you really think I can do this?"

I nod. "I do, Josh. It's okay if you get a little bit of stage fright. All musicians get it. But remember that if someone or something is trying to ruin your performance, most likely it isn't real. And maybe if you can get over your fear of performing in front of an audience, maybe you can start performing in Music again. I'm pretty sure Mrs Hartley will be happy to see you do that again."

Josh smiles. "Okay. I will give this performing thing a go."

I return the smile. "Great. I will let Hailey know and she can discuss it with her brother."

"Hey, Emily, just one more thing before I play some music." He looks away from me for a second, looking down at his guitar. He rests his fingers on the strings and strum a chord before looking at me again. "You know how our family goes to Deighton Falls Campgrounds?"

I nod. Every now and again Josh's parents would take him camping, and they would invite my parents and I along to the trip too. The campground we would go to was a beautiful place that I always enjoyed going to. It was so quiet, hearing the sound of other animals and just being able to get away from the city life, and enjoying nature.

"I was thinking that if it's okay with our parents, I thought that maybe you and I could go there next weekend?"

"Just us?"

Josh nods. "Just us."

I smile, my heart fluttering in my chest at his suggestion. "That sounds good, Josh. Of course I would like to go."

He returns the smile, and then turns his attention to his guitar as he began strumming the strings.

I watch him as he plays one of my favourite Ed Sheeran songs, and sings. I picture Josh on the stage, hearing the audience cheer for joy. He was going to do well up there even if he thinks he wasn't.

And spending the weekend alone with him next week made the butterflies dance around my stomach. It will be the first trip we would ever take to be alone without our parents. I couldn't wait.

Maybe then I will tell Josh how I feel about him.

Chapter 10

I wake up feeling great the next morning. Spending the night with Josh on his first night home from hospital really lifted my spirit. It was great to have him home and seeing him feel good about himself after his suicide attempt. After playing his guitar for a few hours, we climb out onto the tree and then lay on the grass in the front yard, staring up at the night sky. We talked about the camping trip we hope our parents will allow us to go on by ourselves. We talk about school and our dreams for the future, as well as the concert Haylie had invited us to. We stay out there for a long time before we decide we should head to bed before our parents check up on us and wonder where we are.

Haylie came over the next day like she had promised. The three of us went out to lunch. It was nice to do something together as we didn't hang out much outside of school, mostly because Haylie has to baby-sit her two younger brothers or she helps her Mum with her candle making business. This Saturday she was free of all duties and thought going out to lunch was something the three of us could do. She tells us too that she had talked with Elijah this morning, and he was okay with the idea of letting Josh perform. It hasn't been confirmed yet. Elijah was going to discuss the idea with his band mates. Hopefully it will be a yes.

Later in the evening Josh and I decided that we will tell our parents about the plans we wanted to do next weekend. I ask my parents if we could have Josh and his parents over for dinner, and they agreed. Dad decided to make a barbecue with beef sausages and hamburgers. Mum went to the store to get the things we might need for tonight. I help my parents get everything ready, rehearsing to what I wanted to say in my head.

"Thank you, Carrie, Steve, for inviting us over," Phillip says as we sit out on the patio. He grabs a bread roll and a sausage. "It's been a while since we had dinner together."

"It was Emily's idea for us to get together tonight," Dad tells him.

"Well, thank you, Emily."

I smile, reaching for my glass of water and take a sip. Josh places a hamburger bun on both mine and his plate, as well as a patty. I thank him. I make up my burger before I decide to tell our parents why I thought we should have dinner together.

"Josh and I would like to ask you something," I say.

Mum swallows the food in her mouth. "What about, sweetie?"

"We have been talking, and we want to go on a camping trip to Deighton Falls next weekend," Josh says. "Just the two of us."

Our parents look among each other as they decide whether

if they should agree to this idea.

Lynn speaks first, shaking her head. "Josh, no. I don't think that would be a good idea. You just gotten out of the hospital."

"Lynn, I will be fine," Josh tells her.

"What if something goes wrong? What if you don't take your medication?"

Josh sighs. "Lynn, I'm eighteen in two months. I will be fine, seriously. I have been dealing with this illness for a year now. I know how important it is to take my medication. I have never skipped it."

"He has a point, Lynn," Phillip tells his wife. "I'm sure it will be perfectly safe to go on this trip themselves."

I nod. "We will be fine up there. It will just be an overnight trip."

Dad rubs his chin. "I think it should be alright."

"Why do you two want to take this trip on your own?" Mum asks.

"It was something I thought we should do together," Josh says. "I was thinking about it while I was at the hospital, and I just feel like I need to get away. I needed to clear my head and I thought it would be nice to take a trip up to Deighton Falls Campgrounds. And I would like to take that trip up there with my best friend."

Our parents sit there for a moment, staring at each other without saying a word. I'm pretty sure they were having some kind of silent conversation between them on what was best for Josh and I. I understood their concerns, but it should be okay, right? I turned eighteen earlier this month, and it wasn't like we were little kids anymore. We have been to the campground numerous of times before, and we knew the dangers there. We will be completely safe.

After what seemed like forever, Phillip finally spoke. "Well, I think it should be fine with the two of you going up there. Just make sure to text or call us once you get there so we know you made it there okay."

Dad nods. "Yes, I definitely agree to that. You kids can go on this camping trip. Just make sure your homework is done on Friday night."

Josh and I smile at our parents.

"Thank you so much," Josh says.

A trip away alone with Josh was something I never really expected us to do, or that it would ever happen. We had talked about travelling together once we finished school, and camping was not what we had in mind. But as I ate my food, I smile, thinking about the trip next weekend. I couldn't wait for it.

And maybe when we are alone, maybe then I will tell him how I feel about him.

Chapter 11

Elijah and his band mates agreed to allow Josh to perform for a moment on their set.

Josh practices for the next few days. He wouldn't even let me come over to hear the song he was practicing, and told me he wanted it to be a surprise on the night. Josh even sat in the music room during lunch to practice. Haylie and I popped around to hear him play outside the classroom. We didn't go in or let him know that we were here because we knew he most likely will stop playing. I couldn't stop smiling as I watch him play the guitar, so happy that Josh was getting this opportunity, and hopefully it will help with his fear of performing in front of others. I know Mrs Hartley will be extremely happy to hear what Josh is doing. She knows Josh has a bright future with performing, and I'm glad she doesn't push him to perform.

On Thursday night Haylie came to pick us up and took us

to the club her brother's band was performing at.

Haylie takes us backstage so Josh could meet with the band.

"Thank you for this opportunity," Josh says after Elijah introduces us to the band. He turns to Haylie. "Especially you, Haylie. I wasn't expecting you to do this for me until Emily told me about it."

Haylie smiles. "No problems, Josh. I thought it would be awesome for you to do this. You never know when you could get this opportunity again."

"Okay, this is what is going to happen, Josh," Elijah says. "We are going to go onto the stage, play a couple of songs. And then I'm going to invite you up. How many songs do you plan to play?"

"Just one song," Josh answers.

"Are you sure you don't want to play a couple? Maybe you could sing a cover with us."

Josh shakes his head. "Thanks, but I'm happy to sing one song."

"Josh is shy when it comes to performing," I explain.

Elijah gives him a small smile. "No worries, mate. Stage fright is normal. We have performed in front of a few audiences and we still get nervous being up on the stage. You're going to do fine."

Josh smiles. "Thanks."

We leave backstage and go out to the main stage, getting a spot near the front.

"How are you feeling, Josh?" I ask him.

"Nervous." Josh shakes his head. "No, paranoid actually. I keep thinking something is going to go wrong. I'm not afraid of stuffing up a chord or forgetting a lyric, but I do worry about my hallucinations coming to ruin it all."

I put a hand on his shoulder. "Like I told you the other day, you will be fine, Josh. Your hallucinations aren't going to ruin it."

"You're going to do great up there," Haylie adds.

Josh nods, watching one of the stage hands set up the stage. Haylie leaves to get us a drink.

"Aspen has been a jerk to me all week," he says once Haylie is gone. "He keeps telling me I'm stupid for doing this."

"You're right," I say. "Aspen is a jerk, and he has no right to bully you like that. He has no idea what he is talking about."

"He has been fighting with Georgia too. She keeps telling him to be nicer to me. She has been encouraging me to do this."

I smile. "Listen to Georgia. She is smarter than Aspen."

Haylie returns with three bottles of water.

"You will never guess who is here," Haylie beams as she hands us our water.

From the way Haylie smiled, I knew it could only be one person. "Jensen Peters?"

She nods. "Yeah, he was over at the bar getting a drink also. He said hi to me and said he was seeing my brother's band."

I smile at my friend. "That's great, Haylie."

"Did he ask you out?" Josh asks, unscrewing the lid of his bottle and taking a sip.

"Ha ha ha," Haylie says. "Very funny, Josh. No, he didn't ask me out. He didn't say much."

"Well, I guess tomorrow at school you have something to talk to him about," I say with a wink.

The smile doesn't leave Haylie's lips. "I guess I do."

The lights soon dim, and the opening band starts. They are a trio, and they played great music. I keep my eyes on Josh, making sure he is okay. He bobs his head to the music. I smile, glad that Haylie had invited us along here tonight.

Jensen joins us, along with his friends. Haylie's face was beaming with him beside her, and I really hope by the end of the night that Jensen would ask her out. With her crushing on him for months, all I wanted was for her to get her wish being able to go out with him.

Half an hour went by quickly, and the opening band finishes up. The lights return to normal as we wait for Elijah's band to come on. Haylie talks to Jensen, and I really didn't care that she was ignoring me at the moment as she put all attention on him. I was happy for her. Months of being scared to open her mouth to him, she was finally doing it.

Josh then grabs my wrist, squeezing it tightly. I turn to him, trying to get him to let me go. He wasn't looking at me. He stares at the floor, breathing heavy as a panic attack hits him. Oh no.

I need to calm him before he completely loses it.

I pull him aside. "Josh, it's okay."

He shakes his head, still not looking at me. "I can't do it, Emily."

"Do what?" I shake my hand out of his grip.

He looks at something behind me. Aspen. It has to be him.

I rest a hand on his cheek, making him look at me. He's trying to fight against my touch, still refusing to look at me as his eyes is filled with fear.

"Josh, look at me."

Finally, he does. He takes a few deep breaths as he did.

"What's the matter, Josh? Did Aspen say something?"

He doesn't answer me straight away. "I-I can't go up on stage."

"Why not?"

"Everyone will laugh at me. They will tell me I'm no good."

"Who is telling you that, Josh? The voices or Aspen?"

"Both."

"Ignore those voices, Josh. You always said that when you play the guitar, the music is able to help distract you from them. So when you get up onto the stage, you can do the exact same thing."

He nods.

"And as for Aspen, ignore the jerk. He isn't real, Josh. All he wants to do is bring you down. Don't listen to him, okay? He doesn't know what he is talking about. You can do it. When Elijah calls you up, ignore everyone in the room. Keep your eyes on me, and you should be fine. If Aspen or any of your other hallucinations want to show up, or if any of the voices say something, close your eyes for a second, count to ten and then focus your eyes on me. Can you do that, Josh?"

He takes a few deep breaths before saying, "Okay."

I smile at him. "You can do it, Josh. And if you have stage fright, it's going to disappear once you get up there. No one is going to hate your music. I have heard your music, and you're good. They are going to love whatever song you decide to play. And if you ever decide you want to become a musician, you will need to get past your fear of performing."

His breathing begins to relax, returning a smile. "You're right, Em."

"It's going to be alright, Josh. I will be right here with every step of the way."

"Hey, is everything alright?" I turn to see Haylie walking over to us.

I drop my hand from Josh's cheek, and nod. "Yeah, everything is okay. Josh just had a bit of a panic attack."

Haylie turns to him, looking at him with concern. "Are you okay, Josh?"

"Yeah, stage fright. That's all. Emily got me to calm down."

She smiles. "That's good. They should come out on stage soon."

"So," I say with a smile on my face, "you and Jensen."

Haylie's smile spread wider. "I can't believe he is even talking to me."

"It's about time you spoke to him," Josh says.

"I know. Hopefully we can talk again and that this is not a one-off thing."

"Get his number later," I suggest.

"I definitely will."

We join Jensen and his friends. Haylie is still chatting away, while Josh takes my hand. We stand there in silence as we wait for the next set to start.

After fifteen more minutes, the lights dim and Breaking Summer walks onto the stage.

Beside me, I'm pretty sure Haylie screams the loudest than anyone in this room, cheering on her brother as the band play their very first song of the night. I'm thankful as the music starts that Josh has calm down and is lost in the music, swaying and bobbing to the beat. I smile at him, glad that he is feeling much better from his panic attack earlier. I just hope he can control the voices and Aspen for the next half hour until it's his turn to go up onto the stage.

When Breaking Summer is half way through their set, Elijah looks over at Josh and mouths, "Ready?"

Josh nods.

Elijah smiles, and turns to the audience. "Tonight we have a special guest who will be coming to join us on stage." He points to Haylie. "My wonderful sister, Haylie, suggested I should let her friend perform." He looks in Josh's direction. "Come on up here, Joshua."

Josh looks at me before he moves. I give him an encouraging smile. He returns the smile, and then made his way up onto the stage. A stage hand hands Josh an acoustic guitar. The rest of the band moves off the side so Josh could have the stage to himself.

He stands in front of the microphone. He searches the crowd before looking down at me. He gives me a small smile and I return it. I take out my phone, ready to start filming his performance.

"Hi," he says into the microphone. The audience is silence as they wait to see what he will do. "My name is Joshua." He gestures to Haylie. "I just want to say thank you to my friend Haylie for suggesting to her brother to allow me to perform tonight. I'm kind of shy about performing in front of others, but I agree to do this and give it a go." He pauses, surveying the area before turning back to me. "The song I'm going to play tonight is a song I had written about my schizophrenia. I don't like to talk about it much with others, but this song means a lot to me. I would also like to dedicate this song to my best friend Emily."

My heart skips a beat when he says this. No wonder he didn't want me to be around while he practiced playing for tonight.

"Emily has been my friend for a very long time," Josh goes on. "She has been there through every up and downs, as well as keeping me positive once I was diagnosed with my illness. This song is called *These Voices*."

Josh takes a breath and then began strumming the chords on his guitar. He looks at me as he began to sing,

The voices find me in the darkest places
The voices become the things I shouldn't hear
The voices become the things I shouldn't see
I do everything that I can to block them,
To stop myself from losing control of what's really real and
what's not
But when I see you,
You become the light that I need to guide me through the
dark and twisted places

These voices are all that I can hear
These voices tell me things I don't want to hear
Please take me by the hand,
Tell me that everything is going to be alright.
Because tonight the only voice I want to hear is yours

Tears fill my eyes as Josh plays the song. Every lyric he sang, I could feel the pain, the frustration and the fear he goes through every day with his illness. Aspen was being a real dick to Josh earlier, but Josh fought through his negative comments to get up onto the stage to perform tonight. I can imagine how proud Mrs Hartley would be if she could see him up on the stage. It was good practice for him as his last assignment for his HSC he would have to perform in front of his teacher, as well as HSC markers. He wouldn't be allowed to record his performance. I made a note to myself to show his teacher the video on my phone of him.

The audience broke out in a round of applause as he ended the song. Josh's face was lid up like a Christmas tree, proud of himself for listening to me and not letting the voices or for Aspen to stop him from achieving something he enjoys.

Breaking Summer comes back on the stage and the stage hand takes the guitar from Josh.

"Give Joshua another round of applause," Elijah says.

The audience breaks into a cheer.

Elijah turns to Josh. "Great performance, Josh. Are you sure that's the only song you would like to perform? You're welcome to join us on stage to perform a cover."

Josh looks out at the audience as they cheer, wanting to hear more from him. Josh meets my eyes, and I can see the excitement in them, but it was also mixed with fear. What the fear was about, I wasn't sure.

He turns to Elijah, who holds out the microphone to him. "Thanks very much, Elijah, but one song is enough for me. Thank you again for inviting me up on the stage."

Elijah smiles. "It's no problem, Josh."

Josh walks off the stage. Elijah turns back to the audience, announcing the next song they will play. I watch Josh walk down the stage stairs towards me. As soon as he reaches me, I embrace him.

"Thank you for dedicating the song to me," I say as loud as I could over the music, resting my chin on his shoulder. "The song was great."

"No problems, Emily."

He pulls away from me as Haylie walks over to us. She opens her arms and hugs Josh.

"You were great, Josh!" she shouts.

"Thanks again, Haylie, for doing this for me," he says.

Haylie pulls away. "No problems. I just thought it would be something you would like to do with everything that had happened."

Josh smiles brightly.

For the rest of the night, the three of us stand close together, cheering on Elijah and his band.

* * *

Haylie drops us off later. Josh and I stand on my front lawn, talking before we head inside. I couldn't stop smiling, and neither could Josh.

"You did a great job up there tonight, Josh," I say. I hid my hands in the pockets of my hoodie. "I'm proud of you."

"I couldn't have done it without you, Emily."

"You probably could have. You just have to be strong over your voices and any hallucinations who want to bring you down, like Aspen."

Josh nods. "He wasn't there. But the voices were. They kept telling me that everyone was going to hate me and that even you were going to hate me. I did what you told me to do and I kept my eyes on you, and the voices disappeared."

I smile, reaching out to put my hand on his arm. "I'm glad to hear that, Josh. And those voices don't know what they are talking about because I will never hate you. The song was great. I really enjoyed it."

Josh smiles brightly, taking my hands into his. "I'm glad you did, Emily. The song meant a lot to me with what I go through every day."

His palms felt warm against my own.

"Do you think you will be able to perform again like that?"

He shrugs. "I don't know. I think so."

"I hope it's okay, but I'm going to show Mrs Hartley your performance. She will be so proud of you."

He nods his approval. "Yeah, you can show her."

I let go of his hands, tucking a strand of my hair behind my ear that escaped my ponytail. "So I have been thinking to ask Mrs Hartley if I can sit in when you have to perform for her and the HSC markers in a couple of weeks. You know, just in case you freak out during your performance. But if you don't need me there and you feel confident to get out in front of everyone like you did tonight, then that's good. You just need to do your best to block out the voices and hallucinations. Especially Aspen."

"I will see. Thank you, Emily."

I smile. "You're welcome, Josh."

He returns the smile. We stand there for what seemed like forever, staring at each other. We stood close. So close that all I had to do was close a gap between each other and kiss him. It was the perfect moment to do so. A voice in the back of my head was telling me to do it, but I just couldn't bring myself to do it.

"I will see you tomorrow at school," I say instead of taking the leap to kiss him. "Good night, Josh."

"Good night, Emily."

I turn and head up my lawn. When I reach the door, I look back at Josh. He was still standing there out front, watching me until I was safely inside. I wave to him and he returns it. I open the door and enter inside.

You're stupid, Emily, I say to myself. *You should have kissed him. It was the perfect moment.*

I know it was. I don't think I was quite ready for that moment yet.

Maybe, just maybe, things will change between us on the camping trip.

Chapter 12

I show Mrs Hartley the video the next day at school during lunch. She smiles through the whole video.

"This is great, Josh," she says as she hands the phone back to me. "I'm very proud of you for doing this."

Josh smiles. "Emily helped me through it. Honestly, I almost didn't do it, but she encouraged me to."

She turns to me with a smile. "You're a good friend, Emily." She turns back to Josh. "How do you think you are going to go with your performance for the HSC markers in a couple of weeks? I will be speaking to everyone in class next week about it."

Josh shrugs. "I don't know yet."

"I thought that maybe I could be in the room just in case Josh needs to focus on someone or an object, just like I told him to do last night," I tell Mrs Hartley. "He kept his focus on me and that's what got him through the performance."

She pressed her lips together in a thin line as she nods. "I will see, Emily. I'm don't think that is going to be allowed. Maybe before the performance, I can have Josh come practice in front of me, see how he goes with me in the room. But if he still isn't quite comfortable performing in front of just me, then I will put a request in to have you in the room." She turns to Josh. "Does that sound alright to you, Josh?"

"Of course," Josh answers. "I will give it a go, Mrs Hartley."

She smiles. "You will do fine during the exam. From this video, I can already see you will do well. You have nothing to fear, Josh."

We thank her, and headed back to Hailey to have our lunch. And like Mrs Hartley said, Josh was going to do fine during his exam. I'm sure the HSC markers will enjoy his performance.

Josh just needs to get past his fear, believe in himself, and most importantly, ignore the voices and his hallucinations to what they tell him.

* * *

"I'm really surprise your parents are allowing you to go on this camping trip with Josh," Hailey says where she sat on my bed, watching me fold up some clothes to take with me for Josh and my camping trip tomorrow. "My parents will *never* allow me to go on one if a guy is going to be on the trip too."

"I guess maybe because they trust us, and we have known each other for a long time." I put a couple of t-shirts in the bag. I know I didn't need that many, but I really didn't know what to wear. At least I had a few options when I'm on the trip. In a low voice, I say, "But I know if I told my parents I have feelings for

Josh, they might change their minds about us going together."

"You never told them? Okay, maybe not your dad because I really wouldn't tell my dad about my crushes, but my mum I usually do."

I shake my head. "No, I never told my mum either. I have always been afraid to tell her. We may talk about everything, but I have never really told her how I felt about Josh." I move my duffle bag out of the way and sat down next to Haylie. "It's something I haven't been able to tell anyone about, except for you. I have always been afraid to what people might say."

Haylie smiles. "And I'm glad you told me. You also shouldn't fear what people say. It's always exciting to hear who someone is interested in. Do you think you will tell him for real this time during the trip?"

It was a question I still couldn't answer. I keep telling myself I will, but I know I will most likely chicken out and change my mind again.

"Maybe." I bite my lip. Why was it so hard for me to tell Josh how I felt? "I don't know."

"You should tell him, Emily. You never know how he feels until you tell him. Maybe he likes you too, and is shy to tell you, thinking you won't return the same feelings as well."

My thoughts replay the moment last night after she had dropped us off, how close Josh and I stood near each other. We could feel something there, but neither of us wanted to tell each other about it. Like we were scared to be open about it. I haven't told Haylie about it, how there was something between us that none of us was making a move.

Maybe this time one of us will.

Getting off the bed, I pick up another t-shirt and put it in the bag. "Yeah, maybe I will tell him over the weekend."

"No, not 'maybe I will'. It's 'I definitely will.'"

"Okay." I pick up my pyjamas and put it in my bag. "I definitely will tell him. You're happy?"

"I will once you call me to say you admitted it. Better yet, you kissed him!"

I smile, imagine what it would be like if we did kiss. I picture us by the camp fire, he cupping his hands around my jaw and leaning in slowly to kiss me. Or maybe it won't be beside the camp fire. Maybe it will be in the forest or somewhere that will be magical.

But then again, that's if I'm brave enough to tell him how I feel.

"I promise I will let you know if we do." I pick up a jumper next and put it in the bag.

"So, Jensen asked me out today," Haylie suddenly says.

Glancing up when she said this, I see the wide smile on her face. I return the smile. "Oh my gosh, really?"

Haylie's eyes lit up with delight. "He did. We're going to go out to the movies tomorrow."

"That's great!" I hug my friend. "I'm so happy for you, Haylie."

Haylie pulls away. "Hey, if my date goes well and you admit your feelings towards Josh, maybe some time we could all go on a double date."

I nod, unsure if that's something Josh would be comfortable with, but I didn't want to disappoint Haylie. "That sounds good."

I finish packing as Haylie and I keep talking about school, the weekend and about the guys we liked. The whole time we packed, I thought about Josh, even glance a few times over in his room. He wasn't in there, probably downstairs doing something with Lynn or Phillip. I couldn't help wonder what this camping trip could really mean for us. Will we continue being friends or would we become more than that? Does Josh even share the same feelings as me?

Whatever happens, I couldn't wait for the weekend.

Chapter 13

I still couldn't believe that I was going on this camping trip alone with Josh. It's the first time our parents have allowed us to do it. Lynn is overprotective of Josh, constantly worried about whether or not Josh is taking his medication, and I was glad she trusted Josh enough to go on this camping trip without any adult supervision. Even with adult supervision, she worries. Like when Josh and I went on a school camp last year. She spoke to the teachers going on the camp for hours, making sure they knew the importance of Josh taking his medication. They told her everything will be okay, and it was. And she had nothing to worry about this trip either.

Dad had allowed me to take his car, telling me to drive safely and to have a good time. He also told me to call him if I need anything. I told him everything was going to be fine.

Once out on the road, I could feel this sense of freedom

now that I'm off my learner's. Like I could go anywhere on this open road, and I couldn't wait to be able to do this more often. With the radio blasting in the car, everything felt right with it being just Josh and I.

Josh winds the window down, closing his eyes as he lets the cold air come through the window, his hair blowing about in the wind.

"Josh!" I shiver from the cold. "You're letting all of the cold air in. Close the window."

Josh laughs and closes it. "Sorry. I just like the feel of the wind on me. Hey, we should stop for snacks."

I agree to do so as I had to fill the car. I pull into the nearest petrol station. Dad had given me some money for petrol, as well for food Josh and I might want to get even though Mum and Lynn had both gone shopping for us. Mum had brought a small can of baked beans for me. Josh doesn't eat beans, so Lynn had brought a loaf of bread for us and some frankfurts.

Walking into the petrol station to pay, I find Josh in the confectionery aisle. He had picked up a few bags of lollies. As I join him in the aisle, he grabs a bag of marshmallows off the shelf and holds it up at me.

"Hey, Em, we definitely need marshmallows," he says. "We can't go camping without marshmallows."

I smile. "They'll be perfect around the camp fire tonight."

We pay for the stuff. Josh also got himself a slushie before we got back on the road. We talk and sang along with the radio. It felt good to be alone with Josh.

After an hour and a half of driving, we reach our destination. We weren't the only ones here at the campground. There was a family of four there also. I parked the car in a spot we have chosen, and take our stuff out of the car. Josh started setting up the tent.

"You will be alright with the tent?" I ask him.

He nods. "I'll be alright. I've helped Phillip countless of times with setting this tent up."

I give him a hand anyway so he didn't think he had to get it up himself. Once the tent was up, we set up the sleeping bags inside the tent, and we also put our stuff inside too.

"Hey, let's take a walk," Josh says as we climb out of the tent. "What about lunch?"

Josh takes my hand. "We have plenty of time. Let's go exploring and then we will come back to eat."

Josh's palm feels warm against mine as we leave the campground and take a walk down a trail leading down to the waterfall. Deighton Falls was a peaceful place and I loved it how our families came up here every once in a while. It was a great place to visit when you wanted to get away from the city.

We reach the lookout, standing at the fence of the cliff side, and glance over at the waterfall. With the reflection of the sun, I get a glimpse of a small rainbow on the waterfall. There's a cool breeze, but I wasn't going to let the cold air ruin my time here with Josh.

We stare out at the falls and the landscape of the mountains. Somewhere nearby I hear cockatoos squawking, and a kookaburra laughing.

I look over at Josh who was lost in his own thoughts as he stares out at the scenery. I pull out my phone and snap a picture of him. He turns in my direction when he hears the click, smiling. I snap another picture.

"Come here," he says, grabbing my arm and pulls me closer to him until my back was press against his chest. "Let's take a picture together."

Josh takes the phone from me, holding it up high so we could get into the frame. His free arm is wrapped around me, and I hold onto his arm as we smile into the picture. Josh snaps it and hands it back to me.

"I really love it up here," I say, slipping the phone back into the pocket of my jeans, resting my head on Josh's shoulder as he keeps his arm around me.

"Same here."

"What made you decide to come up here for the weekend with it just being the two of us?" I ask him as I turn to face him.

Josh turns to look at me. "I just thought of everything that had happened, it would be nice to get away and spend it with my best friend. I thought going camping would be good. I wasn't sure how we were going to convince our parents to allow us to come up here alone, but I'm glad they did." He smiles.

I return the smile. "I'm glad too."

* * *

We stay out on the trail for a little while longer, skipping lunch, before heading back to camp. The sun was starting to set and the temperature was dropping. I had to throw on an extra jacket to stop me from shivering so much. Josh starts the fire, and we sit beside it, where we make hot dogs to eat for dinner.

"This is nice," I say once we've settled down with our dinner. "Just the two of us and a break from our parents."

Josh nods, taking a huge bite of his hot dog. He swallows it quickly before speaking. "It is. Do you know how annoying Lynn can be some times?" He clears his throat and then imitated Lynn's voice. "'Have you taken your medication, Josh?' 'Josh, don't forget to take your medication.'" He shakes his head.

"She worries about you, that's all. She wants to make sure that you're going to be okay."

"I know. I don't want to feel hassled by her all the time."

"Well, for tonight, you can relax without her nagging you. Just do make sure you take your medication."

He nods. "I have. Don't worry too much about me."

He finishes off his hot dog and then reaches for the bag of marshmallows that is next to his feet. He waits for me to finish my food before opening the bag and holding it out to me.

"Marshmallow?"

I take one from the bag. We pick up long sticks that were near us and stuck the marshmallows at the end of the sticks, putting them over the fire.

"Do you remember the last time we were here, I think just before you were diagnosed with schizophrenia, and you kept hearing this growling sound?" I say to Josh, watching the fire roast my marshmallow.

Josh nods, removing the stick from the fire. He blows on the marshmallow and then pulls it off the stick, popping it into his mouth. I do the same with mine.

"I remember. What did I say it was? A bear?"

I laugh at the memory. "Yeah, you thought it was a bear, and I said that we didn't have bears here. So you said it could have been a koala bear." I shake my head with a smile. "Koalas aren't even bears."

Josh laughs. "I remember. But little did I know at the time that I was the only person who could hear the sound."

Josh looks around into the darkness of the forest. Somewhere an owl hoots, which makes Josh jump.

"You heard that, right?" he asks me.

I nod. "Yes, the owl is real."

We grab another marshmallow each and roast them.

"How do you think Hailey is going with her date?" Josh asks me.

"I reckon she will do well with Jensen," I say as I pull my stick away from the fire. "Hailey will talk non-stop about him on Monday."

I blow on the marshmallow and take it off the stick, popping it into my mouth. Josh does the same with his.

"It's about time she went out with him," Josh says. "I hope the date goes well for her."

"Same here."

I knew that right now could be the perfect time to confess to Josh how I felt about him. What could go wrong if I confessed it? I don't think Josh will stop being my friend because I had feelings for him. We were alone out here. No one could stop me from speaking up except for me.

I have to tell him before I lose my chance again.

I inhale a deep breath and then let out a shaky one.

"Josh, do you ever think about us?" I ask.

He looks my way, surprise to hear me say that. "Of course I do. I always think about us."

I shake my head. "No. I mean, do you ever think of us as more than just friends?"

Josh doesn't look at me, keeping his eyes on the fire. He turns his head slightly to something on his right and I wonder if it's one of his hallucinations. Georgia perhaps. I can imagine what she must be saying to him right now with the conversation I have suddenly brought up.

When Josh doesn't respond to my question, I began to feel stupid for even bringing this conversation up. I shouldn't have said anything. *This* is why I never wanted to say anything to him about my feelings. Now that I have brought up that I like him and that it's obviously he doesn't share those feelings as me, will we be able to forget I ever brought up this conversation?

"I'm sorry, Josh," I say. "I didn't mean to ask you this question. Forget I even asked you this."

I turn away, looking at the fire.

"Don't feel bad for asking me that, Emily."

I force myself to look at him.

"The truth is, Emily, is that yes I do think about us. All the time I wonder what will happen if we became more than that. I always thought we will only be friends and nothing more."

My heart skips a beat after hearing this.

"You like me more than a friend?" I ask.

Josh nods. "I do. I just never knew how to tell you how I felt."

I give him a smile. All this time I was stupidly hating myself about telling Josh how I felt, and all this time he too felt something towards me. We just never made a move because we both were afraid of losing our friendship.

"I like you, Josh," I tell him. "A lot."

Josh stares at me for a long time before reaching out to stroke my cheek.

"I like you too, Emily."

Josh cups his hands around my jaw. He then slowly moves towards me, causing my heart to race a million miles per hour. I meet him half way, closing my eyes as my lips press against his. It's soft and slow. He tastes like marshmallows.

Josh pulls away slightly, looking at me as if to make sure I was okay with this in case I changed my mind. But I hadn't. My lips crave for more of him, and I lean in to kiss him again. I move closer to him as Josh keeps one hand on my jaw and places the other one on my lower back, pushing me closer to him.

My body goes crazy from Josh's touch. This is what I have wanted for a long time. I rest a hand on the back of his neck.

We kissed for what seemed like forever. When we finally pull apart, my head feels like it was spinning. Butterflies dance happily around my stomach. I rest my head on his shoulder and he rests his head on mine.

"Emily," Josh says.

"Yeah?"

"I'm glad to have you as my best friend."

I smile, keeping my eyes on the fire. "I am too, Josh."

"Do you want me to get out my guitar and play some music?"

"That would be great."

Chapter 14

You know how you often have a nightmare that feels so real, but you haven't quite woken up from it? Well, that's how it felt when I woke up the next morning. Only I was fully awake. In fact, I don't even know how to describe the emotions I'm feeling.

I wanted to believe it was all just a crazy nightmare, but the shivering feeling I had wasn't from the cold. When I woke up, Josh's sleeping bag beside me was empty. It wasn't normal for him to wake up before me and I had a gut feeling that something was wrong.

I get up, slipping on my shoes and climb out of the tent, expecting to see Josh cooking breakfast. Only the camp site is empty

"Josh?" I call out to him.

Josh doesn't respond.

I look around, wondering where Josh could be. Perhaps he had gone to the toilet. I grab my phone and then walk towards the restrooms. It's so quiet this morning besides kookaburras laughing in the trees nearby.

I stand outside the male restroom. "Josh? Are you in there?" He still didn't respond.

I pull out my phone and message him. *Hey, where are you at?*

I wait. Minutes pass, but there's still no reply.

I head back to camp. The family sharing our camp site are up and preparing breakfast.

Back at camp, I check the tent again to see if Josh had come back, but he hadn't. An awful feeling in the pit of my stomach rises. I tell myself not to worry, that Josh was nearby somewhere. I mean, it's not like him to disappear without telling me. He would always stay with me until I wake up.

Only this time he hasn't stayed.

Where would he have disappeared to?

I look down at the dirt, hoping that maybe I will be able to see his footprints and that will be able to tell me where he had gone to. There are footprints stamped in the dirt that I do hope belongs to Josh. I follow them and from the looks of it, he must have gone for a walk. Maybe he couldn't sleep, as sometimes he experiences insomnia from his medication, and had gone for a walk. But I doubt he would go out into the bush in the middle of the night. Josh hates the dark. He may not be able to see his hallucinations, but he can hear them.

"Josh, can you hear me?" I call out again. "Where are you?"

I try not to think anything bad as I kept walking, looking everywhere I could see where he could be. Did he go off trail? No, Josh wouldn't do that. Did he climb a tree? No, Josh was terrible at climbing.

"Josh, this isn't funny," my voice shakes. "Where are you?"

I continue down the trail until I reach the lookout. I can hear the waterfall. Josh's footprints go all the way to the railing. I stop short before I walked any further, an uneasy feeling in the pit of my stomach. I look around the lookout, but I couldn't see Josh anywhere. The footsteps don't even show that he had moved from the railing.

No. Please no.

I slowly walk over to the railing, afraid of what I would find if I go any further. I force myself to look over the railing. There, at the bottom of the rocky cliff near the bottom of the waterfall is Josh. His body is lifeless, blood splattered on the rocks beside his head, and his limbs are in angles that aren't normal.

"Josh!" I let out a piercing scream.

I look around for a way down. There have to be stairs or a trail leading somewhere down to the waterfall. I find the stairs and run down them, almost tripping. I reach Josh, lifting his head and resting it in my lap. His eyes are closed. No sign of any life in him as I beg for him to wake up.

No. This can't be happening. No.

This is all just a horrible nightmare I haven't woken up from. I'm sure of it.

He didn't jump, did he? He promised he wouldn't do something like this to me again!

I press my fingers to his neck, his skin cold. There's no pulse.

No, no, no!

My body trembles as I sob hard, not wanting to believe Josh is dead.

This is all a nightmare. Josh is alive. I'm dreaming and any minute now I will wake up and Josh will be sitting next to me in the tent, alive.

But no matter what I do to tell myself to wake up, Josh is still lying there on the ground, lifeless.

Why Josh? Why did you do this? Especially with the great time we had last night. I thought he had gotten the help he needed so he wouldn't do this again. He promised me he wouldn't try to take his life again.

I sit there for what seems like forever, my body frozen from the shock.

Finally, I pull my phone out of my pocket and press my mum's number.

"Hey, Emily, how's the camping trip?" she asks when she answers.

At the sound of my mother's voice, I burst into tears.

"Emily? Emily, what's wrong?" Mum's voice is full of concern.

I sniff. "Josh... Josh is..." I can't even say the word. It was much too painful to say it.

Mum says something next but I don't hear her words as I began sobbing again. I don't even notice my Mum had hung up the phone until I hear the dial tone.

"Hey, is everything alright?"

I look up to see where the male voice was coming from. Up on the lookout, peering over the edge was the father from the camp site near us. I shake my head. He moves away and within minutes he was at my side.

"I heard screaming," he says. "Is everything alright? What happened?"

I was surprised he had heard me screaming. I didn't think it would be heard from the campground.

The man kneels down beside me, resting a hand on my

back and reaches for Josh's neck. He curses when he doesn't feel a pulse. He fishes out his phone from his pocket.

"Can you tell me what happened?"

I shake my head. "I... I don't know. I found him like this. I... I think he might have jumped."

The man pats my back as he calls triple zero.

"Everything is going to be alright," he tells me.

No. Nothing is going to be alright.

Josh is dead. My best friend. The boy who I have loved was gone.

* * *

The man stays with Josh and I until the paramedics came. Even when they came and started asking me questions, I couldn't answer them. I couldn't move. The world around me had stopped. I had to force myself to say what I think might have happened. I watch as Josh's body was put in a bag and then was lifted up. The man helps me up and we follow the paramedics back to camp where the ambulance was parked. The man's family was nearby, watching. He leaves me alone at my camp site and walks over to them.

Two cars pull up into the camp site, but I don't look to see who had arrived. I keep my eyes on the paramedics as they place the sketcher in the back of the ambulance. It's then I see Lynn and Phillip running over to the ambulance. Lynn breaks down and Phillip comforts his wife. Mum and Dad hurries past them and over to me.

"Emily, I'm so sorry." Mum throws her arms around me. I don't react to her hug straight away as I kept my eyes on the ambulance.

"Everything is going to be okay, Emily." Dad hugs me once Mum pulls away and I wrap my arms around his shoulders, holding onto him tightly.

I wanted to tell Dad that everything wasn't going to be okay. Nothing will ever be alright. I have lost my best friend, the boy I loved, who had committed suicide while I was asleep. I don't see how everything is going to be okay. My world had stopped and was crumbling around me. My heart breaks to pieces in my chest.

Last night everything was great. We laughed, sing and shared our first kiss. What went wrong after that? Why did Josh take his life? I thought he had gotten all the help last week while he was in the hospital.

"Let's get you home," Dad says.

He turns to my mother, telling her he will take me home. She agreed and said she will pack everything up and then drive back home in the car I had driven. Dad lifts me up and carries me to the car.

Lynn rushes over to Dad and me as we walk by the ambulance, where she was clinging to her husband and sobbing into his shoulder. Phillip follows her. She frowns at me. "This is *your* fault, Emily. I told you I didn't want you and Josh to come up here on your own."

"Lynn, don't," Phillip tells his wife, putting a hand on her shoulder.

My heart crushes in my chest. How could Lynn Hopkins blame me for Josh's death? Josh was the one who wanted to do this camping trip. This wasn't even supposed to happen.

"Hey! Lay off, Lynn!" Dad scolds at her. "This isn't Emily's fault. She didn't know Josh was going to do this. And it was his idea to come on this trip. Not my daughter's, so don't you dare put the blame on her."

Thank you, Dad, I say silently to myself.

Lynn nods, pressing her lips into a thin line. "You're right, Steve. I'm sorry, Emily. I didn't mean to blame you."

I don't say anything in response.

"Listen," Dad says to the Hopkins, "I'm going to take Emily home. Carrie is going to pack everything up. I'm also very sorry about Joshua."

Phillip gives Dad a small smile. "Thank you, Steve." He puts a hand on my shoulder. "I'm sorry, Emily."

Dad walks away from the Hopkins and heads towards the car. He opens the back passenger seat, and settles me down. He puts the seat belt over me. I rest my head against the window once he closes the door and heads to the driver's side. Josh is all I can think about as Dad starts the car and pulls away from the campgrounds.

I think about what Lynn had said back there. Was it really my fault that Josh was dead? Should I have not agreed to come up here without our parents? If we hadn't gone camping, would he still be here?

"Dad, is it true what Lynn said?" I say, finally managing to open my mouth to speak. "Is it really my fault that Josh is dead?"

My father looks at me through the review mirror. "No, it isn't, Emily. Lynn didn't mean to say what she said."

Of course she didn't. She had to blame someone for his death. Why not blame me?

"If we didn't go on this camping trip, do you think Josh will still be alive?"

Dad doesn't answer me straight away. "I honestly don't know, Emily."

"Josh didn't even want to die! He told me he didn't. I don't understand why he would do this. He promised me he would not try to attempt suicide again!"

I burst into tears. Why did this happen? Why didn't I wake up when Josh snuck out of the tent? I could have stopped him. I *should* have stopped him. He would still be here if I had stopped him.

Dad pulls onto the side of the road and gets out. He opens the back door on his side and hops in. He unbuckles my seat belt and pulls me into his lap, hugging me. With my father's arms around me, I didn't want to let go of him at all.

Chapter 15

As soon as Dad and I got home, I climb the stairs to my room. I barely even remember the trip home. I closed the door to my room and glance over in Josh's room. I expected to see him there, but then I had to remind to myself he was no longer living next door to me. Everything felt quiet and still. It felt like time had stop without Josh being here.

I closed the blinds so I couldn't see into his room. I curl up onto my bed, not wanting to move from it at all. I wanted Josh to be here beside me and snuggle up to me. I wanted him to talk to me about anything – his hallucinations, school, us, just anything. Most of all I wanted him to tell me I'm dreaming, and when I wake up he will be lying here beside me.

I thought about last night when he had kiss me. Why did he kiss me if he was just going to leave me afterwards? Why did he even bother to tell me he like me only to rip my heart out like this?

Mum comes into my room later to check on me. She sits down beside me on my bed, stroking my hair.

"I just came to say that I'm here if you would like to talk," she tells me. She puts a piece of fold up paper on my bedside table. "I also found a note that Josh had written to you. I'm going to leave it here for you, and you can read it whenever you feel up to it."

All I could do was nod.

Mum stays with me for a few more minutes before leaving me to be by myself.

I stay in my room for three days. I didn't feel up to doing anything, not even talk or eat. I only leave the room to use the bathroom before locking myself in my room again. I keep the blinds closed so I can't glance next door. My room may have been dark, but I didn't care. Haylie had called me a few times and even stopped by to see how I was, but I didn't want to see or talk to her. All I wanted was to be alone and think about Josh. He was the only person running through my mind.

By Thursday my parents said I had to go to school. They didn't want me to be missing out on anymore work or falling behind. I didn't see the point in going when I wasn't even going to be able to concentrate on anything. Let alone having everyone tell me they are sorry for my loss or constantly asked me if I'm okay. Gabby was one person I wasn't looking forward to seeing. I didn't want to know what she had to say about all of this.

Plus, my parents had made an appointment for me with the school counsellor, Mrs Roberts. Even when I told them I was fine, they suggested I go and talk with her.

Mum drops me off at school. Haylie stood there waiting for

me. She greets my Mum and once she drives away, Haylie pulls me into a hug.

"I miss you so much, Em," she says. "I couldn't stop thinking about you, and hoped you would return to school soon."

"I miss you too, Haylie," I say, resting my chin on her shoulder. "I'm sorry for not talking to you in the last few days."

"It's okay. I absolutely understand why and that you just needed your space. I'm here if you ever want to talk. I'm so sorry, Emily."

I pull away from her, and glance at the cars passing by or pulling up to the kerb to drop off students. I keep looking for Lynn's car, like she will pull up any second and Josh will get out of the car. But of course she wasn't coming. Neither was Josh.

Haylie rests a hand on my shoulder. "Come on, let's go."

* * *

Maths was not a subject I wanted to deal with first period. But what choice did I have? It wasn't like I could tell my teacher to let me sit out of this class because that will never happen. If I had any choice at all, I would still be locked in my room, hiding from the world as time stopped. Yet, I had to be in school. Three days was enough for my parents to allowed me to skip school, but it didn't feel like it was enough for me.

I sit at my desk while Mr Carlson talks about something that I had drifted off the moment he walked into the classroom. As he talked, I stare at Josh's seat. If he was here, he would be listening to our teacher carefully, taking notes and answering maths equations with ease. My heart sinks low in my chest. It felt strange without him being here. This classroom didn't feel the same without him here.

Nothing felt the same anymore. All I have is a missing hole in my heart.

My thoughts were soon interrupted when I heard Mr Carlson calling my name. I turn to face him. Everyone in the class turn to look at me as well. At first I thought I was in trouble for not listening to a word my teacher was saying, but I wasn't in trouble. I saw a student walk out of the classroom and I realise it was a student on office duty, probably fetching me to go and see Mrs Roberts, who I still didn't want to see.

Mr Carlson tells me to grab my stuff and hands me a note to tell me that I'm required to see the counsellor. I make eye contact with no one as I leave the classroom. I take my time walking to the office.

I stand outside Mrs Roberts' office and knock on the door. I hear shuffling on the other side and then the door opens, revealing our school counsellor. She greets me with a small warm smile, moving aside and gesturing me inside her office.

"Emily, come on in."

I listen to her, stepping over the threshold and slip my bag off my shoulders. I sit down in front of her desk and rest my bag against my feet.

Mrs Roberts sits down across from me. "Thank you for coming to see me, Emily."

Why thank me when it wasn't even my choice? I say to myself.

"I'm really sorry about Joshua Harman. He was a great student."

Why must I be here and be forced to talk to someone I don't want to talk to? Especially when it's about Josh?

"Yeah," I mumble a soft reply.

"Do you want to tell me what happened on Sunday morning with Josh?" she asks me.

I sit there in silence, staring at the edge of Mrs Roberts' desk. I didn't want to think about Sunday morning. I didn't want to talk about it with anyone. His lifeless body still remained in my head and I couldn't shake it from me. It's not the last thing I wanted to remember Josh by. Will the image ever leave my head?

"Emily, can you please tell me? I understand what you might be feeling. If you can tell me what happen then it might help you to feel better and get everything off your chest."

I nod. I haven't spoken to anyone what had happened since Sunday. Not to my parents or to Haylie. As soon as I open my mouth to speak, tears start filling my eyes. *Why did you do this to me, Josh? Why?*

"I didn't expect him to do that," I choke out. "I really didn't. I thought he had gotten help when he went to the hospital last week. He didn't want to die. If I knew he was going to take his life, I would have stayed up all night to make sure this wouldn't have happened. The same thing I wouldn't have gone to Gabrielle Casey's stupid party if I had known he would have tried to take his life. I don't understand why he couldn't have discussed what he was going through his mind and why he had come to that decision to end his life. He was my best friend. He told me everything. He would talk to me about his hallucinations or any delusions he was having. I can't help it to think that this is my entire fault. I should never have agreed to go on this camping trip with him. His mother said it was my fault when she had heard about his death. Okay, she said it while she was upset, but I still wonder if it was all my fault. She never even wanted Josh to go on this trip. All Josh wanted was to do something with me and be alone. That's all he wanted. And his mother immediately blames me. It was Josh's idea for the trip, and she blamed me!"

I cover my face with my hands. Mrs Roberts was right. Getting out everything that I've kept to myself for the past few days feels like a weight has been lifted off my shoulders. Only it didn't really repair my broken heart and it may never will.

"Emily, look at me."

I remove my hands from my face, wiping at the tears.

Mrs Roberts leans forward in her seat. "Don't blame yourself for Josh's death. It isn't your fault at all. Josh was the one who decided to take his own life, not you or anyone else made him do it."

I nod, knowing she was right. Josh was the one who chose to take his own life. No one else made him do it. Except for maybe the voices in his head that tells him so many things that aren't true. I don't know if they somehow convinced him to do it. If they did, I hate them for it.

* * *

For the rest of the school day, it seemed to have gone slow. I was glad to finally be back at home, away from people who felt sorry for me. Even Ron and Elliot came up to me, apologising to me of all the cruel things they had said and done to him. I never accepted their apology. Why apologise now when Josh was gone? Why not apologise when he was alive?

I lock myself in my room, away from the world. I didn't want to do my homework, but I thought I might as well start it since I knew it will take a while to complete it. It's bad enough I have missed three days of school work. Only my mind just wasn't focus on anything. My maths textbook is open in front of me and all I do is stare at the numbers in the book. My mind became blank as nothing on the page made any sense at all.

I thought back to the other week when Josh came over and had helped me out with my homework. I wish he was right here with me to help me out. I kept glancing over in his room, hoping to see him, that I was still living in this nightmare, and later Josh will come over. He would have hug me, tell me that it was just a dream and he will always be here for me.

I have no idea how long I had been sitting there for, staring at my open textbook and staring into space, when a knock on my door snaps me back to reality. My mother's voice calls out to me from the other side, telling me I have a visitor. She didn't say who it was, and I figured it must be Haylie.

I closed my textbook, knowing I was never going to get anywhere with it. I wonder if Mr Carlson and my other teachers will let me get off easily for not doing my homework. They will understand if I'm not in a good headspace, right?

I walk downstairs to find not Haylie standing at the door, but Lake Terra. He holds a bouquet of pink lilies. I walk over to him, surprised to see him.

"Lake, what are you doing here? How did you know where I live?"

"I asked Haylie where you lived. Sorry for showing up here unannounced."

I shake my head. Why did Haylie tell him where I lived? "No, it's okay. I just wasn't expecting anyone to come over. I haven't exactly wanted any visitors since Sunday."

"I wanted to come see how you are doing. I wanted to talk to you in school, but you didn't really want to talk to anyone."

I step out onto the veranda with him, closing the door behind me. "Well, thanks for stopping by."

Lake holds out the flowers to me. "Here. These are for you. I hope they cheer you up a bit."

I smile, taking the flowers as I thank him. It was a nice gesture he has done, but the flowers didn't cheer me up. It was going to take a lot to make myself feel better again. What would make me happy again if I was able to see Josh's face, to hear his voice and to have his arms around me.

"I know you probably heard this about a hundred million times already, but I just wanted say sorry for your loss. I kind of wish I was nicer to Josh rather than making fun of him like Gabby wanted me to."

"You shouldn't let her control you on how to act towards others."

Lake looks down at his shoes as he nods. "You're right. I shouldn't let her do that to me." He looks up at me. "Well, I should go. Do you know when the funeral is going to be?"

I nod. "Josh's parents have organised it to be on Monday."

"Okay. Thanks for letting me know." He starts to turn, but then turns back to me. "Oh, just one more thing before I go. If you need someone to talk to about Josh, I'm here for you."

I wasn't quite sure if Lake was someone I wanted to talk to about Josh, but I tell him I will keep that in mind.

Lake leaves, walking back to his car parked on the street. I watch him leave.

Once he was gone, I glance down at the flowers, admiring them. I notice a small white card attached to the bouquet. I read it.

To Emily,
I'm sorry for your loss. I will always be there for you when you need someone to talk to.

Lake

Chapter 16

Getting up and out of the bed for the past few days was hard. But Monday was the hardest. I really didn't want to get up and wished I could have stayed in bed.

I lay in bed for a long time, staring out of my bedroom window, thinking of excuses to stay in bed so I didn't have to attend the funeral. But what kind of friend would I be if I didn't attend it?

Giving myself another few minutes before dragging myself out of bed, I headed to the shower to freshen up. For a long moment of time, I stand under the warm water as it cascaded down my body. I have no idea how long it had been but I hardly notice the water turning cold until Mum knocked on the door asking me if everything was okay. Switching off the water, I reply back that it was.

Back in my room I grab the black knee-length dress from

the wardrobe I had chosen to wear and put it on, along with stockings and a grey cardigan. Once dressed, I pull my hair into a ponytail and stare at my reflection in the full-length mirror. Even with a shower to freshen up, I still look like a total mess with the dark lines forming under my eyes from the sleepless nights. I don't know how I can do this. I shouldn't have to do this.

Mum calls me down for breakfast, the smell of scramble eggs and bacon filling the air, but I still haven't had the appetite to eat. I have hardly eaten anything since Sunday. My parents have forced me to eat and I only eat a bit to make them happy. But this morning I just couldn't think about food. Instead of sitting in the kitchen with my parents, I sat on the couch, checking my social media.

I haven't checked my social media for a couple of days. As soon as I logged on, I was greeted by dozens of notifications from people who had left messages on my wall, telling me they are sorry for my loss. Elijah had sent me a private message, telling me he is sorry about Josh and he is here if I ever wanted to talk.

The service for Josh's funeral was held outside. Fold up chairs were place in front of the brown casket. White flowers were out on top of it, along with a portrait of Josh. A few teachers, including the principal, were there, along with some students from our grade. Lake was one of them. Friends and family of Lynn and Phillip arrived. I was glad to see Haylie. I hug her tightly as soon as I see her. She sits with me in the second row where we sat behind Lynn and Phillip. She squeezes my hand tightly, letting me know that everything is going to be alright. My parents sat on the other side of me. Elijah also came and so did the rest of his bandmates. I wasn't expecting them to be here, but it was nice to see them.

The funeral conductor starts the ceremony, talking about Josh. I keep my eyes on the portrait, trying to figure out what was going through Josh's head when he had decided to jump. It still didn't make sense to me to why he had done it. That weekend he was happy to finally be home and to spend time with me. What went wrong after we had gone to sleep that Saturday night? What if I had woken up when he had disappeared? Could I have stopped him from taking his life?

When Josh's casket was being lowered into the ground, I couldn't take it anymore. I choke out the tears and then run off. I couldn't stand there and watch my best friend, the boy that I had loved, be buried.

Sobbing hard, I walk a few metres away towards the road. Tears blur my vision and I didn't go too far. I sit down on the kerb and folded my arms across my lap, burying my face.

"Why did you do this, Josh?" I cry out. "Why? I loved you. You didn't have to go."

I hear footsteps walking over to me, but I don't look to see who it was. Not even when they sit down on either side of me. But I knew it was my mother and Haylie who had come after me. Mum wraps her arms around my shoulders and pull me towards her where I rest my head on her shoulders. Haylie rests a hand on my knee.

"It's okay, Emily," Mum says, rubbing a hand up and down my arm to sooth me.

"I loved Josh," I tell them. "Why did he do this to me?"

"I don't know, sweetie."

"I told him that I liked him and he also liked me. We kissed! Why did he kiss me and then went and take his life?"

My question hangs in the air for a few minutes.

"Maybe it felt overwhelming for him," Haylie answers.

Maybe it was. But it still didn't make any sense to why he did this. I thought he was happy once he had gotten the help he needed and was able to leave the hospital. I thought he was happy to be back at home with me.

Why would he take his own life if he was happy?

"It's my fault that he is dead," I say.

Mum removes her arm from around me and then makes me face her. "Don't ever think that, Emily."

"But it is my fault." I swallow, but it doesn't get rid of the lump that has formed in my throat. "I shouldn't have agreed to go on the camping trip. I shouldn't have fallen asleep. I could have stopped Josh."

Mum presses her lips into a thin line, stroking my hair. "Honey, you can't change what happened. Don't blame yourself for Josh's death. It's not your fault."

This is your fault, Emily. I told you I didn't want you and Josh to come up here on your own, I remember Lynn's words, even if Dad said she didn't mean to say it to me. Her words were still hurtful when I think about it.

"It is my fault, Mum," my voice croaks through my tears. "Lynn said it is. She said if we didn't go to Deighton Falls Campgrounds, Josh would still be here."

Mum shakes her head. "Lynn didn't mean to say those words. She was upset, probably shock from the news, and the first thing she did was blame someone."

My heart stabs itself when Mum says those words. I push her hand away from me. "So the first person she had to blame was me, right? I was there with him so of course it's my fault that he is dead."

"Honey, Lynn didn't mean to say those things. What

happened to Josh wasn't your fault."

"But it feels like it is." I stand up. "I could have done something to stop him. I should have been able to see what he was planning to do."

But I couldn't because Josh never showed any signs that he was going to end his life that night. He was happy, telling stories, laughing and just enjoying being around me. What went wrong that night? Why didn't I notice that something was wrong? I wish I could go back and know what was going through his head. I want to tell him that everything will be okay, that I'll always be there for him no matter what happens.

Mum stands up and pulls me into another hug. I cry into her chest. Haylie hugs me from behind.

"Everything is going to be alright, Emily," Haylie tells me. "We will get through this together."

I nod, glad I wasn't alone in all of this.

Chapter 17

After the funeral, most people headed back to the Hopkins' place. My parents were in the lounge room, talking to the other grown-ups while Haylie and I sat at the kitchen island. Our teachers, principal and the other students had all headed back to school.

I stare at the egg and mayo sandwich that's cut up into small triangles on my plate, along with some fruit and a chocolate tart, barely touching it. I only had a small bite of the sandwich, which was Josh's favourite, but I didn't have the appetite. Haylie, though, was happy to eat her food. She kept encouraging me to eat something, but I just couldn't.

"I'm still surprise that Lake showed up today," Haylie says, taking a bite of her chocolate tart. "I honestly wouldn't expect him to be at the funeral. I figured he would be doing whatever Gabby tells him too."

I nod in agreement. I haven't told her about him being at my house the other day or the flowers he had given me, even though she probably knew already that he had showed up when he asked her where I lived. She just never asked me how it went. Or maybe she was just giving me space and let me be the one to bring it up when I was ready. It was still a surprise to myself how he was no longer listening to Gabby, but I still wasn't sure if I wanted him to get close to me or have him as a friend, even though he has expressed an interest in me. Maybe he has changed since breaking up with Gabby, but still I haven't forgotten all of the things he has done and said about Josh.

"It was nice though that he still came," I say. "He may have changed, but I don't know if I like the idea of him trying to be friendly to me. Like all the things he did or said to Josh with Gabby, being friendly doesn't make up for what you have done to him."

"Definitely. Promise me to be careful around him? There's something about Lake Terra that I don't trust. I mean, his name itself sounds like some kind of horror movie."

I snort. "It kind of does, doesn't it?"

Haylie laughs back. "It does." She goes back to being serious. "But promise me to be careful around him, Em? I don't want to see you get hurt."

I nod. "I promise, Haylie. And tell Jensen that I said thanks for coming to the funeral. Thank Elijah and his band mates for coming too. They hardly know him and it was nice to have them there."

Haylie smiles. "I will tell them. Hey, when this wake is over, why don't we go and do something together? We could catch a movie or go get ice cream?"

I was about to tell Haylie my answer when Lynn and Phillip

walks into the kitchen. They approach us at the island.

"Emily, can we talk to you for a second?" Phillip asks me.

I give them a sad smile, nodding. Haylie stands up from the stool, telling me she will be in the lounge room, and leaves the three of us alone.

"Emily, we just want to say thank you for being Josh's friend, and for always being there for him," Lynn says once Haylie had left the kitchen.

I smile. "No problem."

"If there's something in Josh's room you would like, you're welcome to take it," Phillip tells me.

"Thanks, Lynn, Phillip." I give them a small smile. "I'm sorry for everything that happened. If I knew Josh was going to do this, I wouldn't have gone on this camping trip with him. I'm still trying to wrap my head around it all, trying to figure out what made him jump. He was so excited for the trip, wanting the weekend to be about us."

Lynn hugs me. "Oh, Emily. Don't blame yourself for what happened. It isn't your fault." She pulls away. "I know I had said some things to you and I had blamed you, but I was just shock from the news. I shouldn't have put any blame on you. It was wrong for me to. And I'm sorry. It's just that ever since Josh was diagnosed with this illness, I always made sure he got the help he needed and he was taking his medication. When the two of you decided you want to go on the camping trip on your own, I thought what if something happens and I'm not there to protect him."

I nod, understanding now what Lynn must have been feeling. I give her a sad smile. "I'm sorry I wasn't able to protect him. I just wish in some way I knew what he was going to do, and I would have stop him. But he did it while I was sleeping. I wished I had woken up and followed him."

"We know you did everything you could, Emily," Phillip says. "Even if you couldn't save him, you were always there for him. You were the first friend he made when he first came home with us. You have been there through his ups and downs, especially the things that had happened with his parents. No six years old should have to deal with what he had gone through. And when he was diagnosed with schizophrenia, you could have stopped being his friend. You were with him when he was being bullied because of his illness, and you listened to him when he needed someone to talk to. You're a loyal friend, Emily. Joshua was very lucky to have you."

I thank them. They give me another hug and ask if I will be joining everyone in the lounge room. I reach in my left pocket of my cardigan, where I feel the piece of paper of Josh's letter. I still wanted to be alone, but I told them I will come out soon. They leave the kitchen, and when they are gone, I pull out Josh's letter. I hadn't read it since my mother handed it to me and said she had found it at the camp site. I hesitated about reading it for a long time, and today I knew I needed the answers to why Josh took his life.

Especially after we had shared our first kiss.

I leave my plate of food on the island, and then sneak up the stairs to the second floor to Josh's room so I can be alone. I feel his room would be the best place for me to read his letter.

Walking into his room felt weird. Everything was left the same way when we had left for the camping trip. His bed was neatly made, his school bag sat on the floor at the foot of his bed, and everything else seemed untouched. His guitar was sitting in the corner of his room near his computer desk, which one of his parents had put it there. A large electric guitar wall sticker is above his bed, along with some band posters and quotes about music around his room, some of them starting to peel off from the Blu-Tack. My heart ached. It felt weird to be in here without him.

There were so many memories within this room. We hung out in here to talk or we had done our homework in here. Josh played his guitar for me for the very first time in this room. For months while he was learning it, he didn't want me to hear it, even though I lived next door and could hear him. When he was confident enough to have me listen, he sat me on his bed and played the chords he had learned. There were other times too when we would dance to music in here.

I wish I could go back to those days.

I sit down on his bed, pulling out his letter from my pocket. The paper had been ripped out of a notebook that I didn't even know he had brought along with him. He had folded the A4 lined paper neatly into a square with my name written messy in black ink. I stare at it for what feels like a long time, afraid to know what it might say. But I knew I shouldn't wait any longer. I had to open it to find out why Josh had done this.

Taking a deep breath, I unfold the paper. Seeing my name in the top corner instantly formed a lump in my throat as I choke back tears. As I read, I could hear his voice inside my head like he was right here beside me, reading it to me.

Dear Emily,

By the time you open this letter, I will no longer be here. I'm really sorry you have to wake up and see me like this. This is not the way I wanted you to find me. I know you're wondering why did I take my own life, especially when I had just come out of the hospital to seek help? You probably think I'm selfish for taking my own life and not thinking about anyone else. This is not the way I wanted to leave the world. But I feel it's the only way. I did it because for the past month it has been overwhelming for me. It has been a struggle to live my life the way I want. But sometimes this illness makes me feel trapped, like everyone is out to get me and then there's the things the voices say to me that are sometimes terrifying. It doesn't help when some people look at you, watching your every move because they think you're dangerous.

Emily, you have been my best friend since the day I moved next door. I want you to know I really appreciate you for always being there for me. I will never forget the memories I have shared with you over the years. I have also been secretly in love with you for a few years. I was afraid to tell you, afraid it would ruin our friendship.

I don't want you to read this and think that our kiss ruined our friendship, or it's one of the reasons why I decided to end my life, because it isn't. The kiss was one of the best things that has happened to me with you. The voices in my head told me that I'm making a big mistake, that you will never love me because of the way I am. I know I shouldn't believe anything those voices tell me. But I have been feeling for a while to disappear, like I have become a burden to everyone, and I sometimes do feel like a burden around you. I feel I'm holding you back and you have all of these opportunities ahead of you, that somehow with my illness I will ruin everything for you. You deserve so much better than me. I feel I'm dragging you down and I can't stand to do this to you anymore.

I will always love you, Emily. I want you to know that.
Love Josh

P.S. There is something in my room that I had left for you. There's a black USB stick beside my computer that I want you to have.

I sat there staring at his words, the tears flowing down my cheeks. I want to scream at him that he didn't need to do this, that he was never holding me back. Josh meant the world to me. Why would he do this to me? To everyone around him? I know he struggled so much with the voices in his head, but why did he give in and listened to them?

I fold up the letter and put it back into my pocket. I then sat down at his computer desk where I see the USB sitting beside the keyboard. White tape was on it, my name written on it with a blue ink pen.

His computer was still on and I move my finger around the mouse pad to wake it. I type in his password and the desktop screen came up. A picture of me and Josh with our arms around each other was his background picture, one that we had taken in his room. My lips curl into a sad smile.

I put the USB into his laptop and click on what he wanted me to see. There was a video file on it label *For Emily,* as well as a music file label *These Voices,* the name of the song he had sung on stage at Elijah's gig. I click on the video and Josh pops up on the screen, sitting at his desk with his guitar.

"Hi, Emily," he says. "I wanted to make this video because there's this song I have been working on and I want to dedicate this song to you. You have been my best friend ever since I moved in next door, and I can't thank you enough for always being there for me. I want to also let you know that I love you, and I have been secretly in love with you for a while, I have just been scared to tell you."

He starts playing the chords on his guitar, and I instantly recognise it. *These Voices*. I sit there watching him sing it, thinking about the night he had sang on stage. How he felt so happy being up on stage, and sharing this song to everyone who attended the concert.

When he finishes the song, he says, "I love you, Emily."

He cuts off the video.

I sit there, staring at the computer screen in silence. The hole in my heart was still there. I had hoped to find closure to why Josh had gone and done this. Instead, it left me asking more questions to answers I will never know. I clench my fist together, hoping it will stop me from grabbing something to throw. I wanted nothing more to grab this laptop and smash it across the wall. Why didn't I act sooner on my feelings? Would he had stayed if I'd told him how I felt?

Continuing to stare at the screen, staring at every inch of his facial features, like maybe it would have given some kind of hint on what he had been planning to do in this video. I wonder when he had made it. Did he make this video because he had planned to commit suicide? Did he plan to end his life that night at the campsite, or was it unexpected, something the voice in his head told him to do? Or did he make this video the night of his first suicide attempt?

I unclench my fist, choking out the tears as they fall, thinking all of this time to what Josh has truly felt towards me. We had a shot at being more than friends, and now we will never know.

Why did you do this, Josh? Why?

I wish I could talk to him one last time and tell him that everything will be okay, that we will get through this together. He didn't have to say goodbye for good.

There's a knock at the door, follow by Haylie's voice. "Emily?"

I wipe my eyes. "Come in."

The door opens and Haylie walks in. "Hey, what are you doing in here? Everything okay?"

I nod. I eject the USB and take it out, slipping it into my pocket. "Yeah, everything is okay. I just came in here because Josh's parents said I can take something from here if I want."

Haylie looks around the room. "Are you?"

I shrug. "I don't know yet. The only thing I'm taking is this USB Josh had left me. He recorded the song he sang at your brother's concert." I bite my lip, feeling the tears threatening to fall again.

"Are you up to going out with me to get ice cream? You don't have to, but I just thought we could go and do something. Get away from here for a while."

I smile. "Ice cream sounds good."

Haylie returns the smile. She takes another look around the room, taking in any memories she had in this room before leaving. I go to follow, but before I step over the threshold, I pause to look at Josh's room – maybe for the last time – and closed the door behind me.

Chapter 18

Haylie allowed me to change before heading to her place. While she changed, I waited for her in the kitchen where Elijah was, making himself a protein shake. I thanked him for coming to Josh's funeral. He gives me a warm smile before asking me how school was. I was thankful he didn't ask me how I was doing or anything to do with Josh because it wasn't something I wanted to talk about right now. School wasn't something I wanted to talk about either, but I kindly tell him it was okay, even if right now school was difficult for me with everything that is going on. Moving on about school, we talked about his band and how he had another gig coming up next month, until Haylie returns.

We head into town, heading to the gelato place the three of us had always enjoyed going to. As we enter the store, I try not to think about the memories I had with Josh here. We order our ice creams in a cup – cookies and cream for Haylie and chocolate for me – and sit down at a table to eat it.

"I know it's a school night, but I'm thinking we could have a sleepover at my place tonight," Haylie says. "I'm pretty sure our parents will be okay with it."

A sleepover at Haylie's sounded nice, but I still wanted my space. Haylie may be my friend, but I still haven't been able to fully open up to her about everything that has happened in the past week. I knew she would listen to any concerns about Josh, as he is her friend too, but I just couldn't bring myself to talk about him with anyone.

I didn't know how to tell this to Haylie, though. The last thing I even wanted was to hurt her feelings because I couldn't open up to her. The least I could do is take up on her offer.

I give her a small smile. "Thanks, Haylie, but maybe over the weekend. I don't think any of our parents will agree to it on a school night."

Haylie licks her spoon. "Yes, I know. I just thought it would be worth a try. Do you want to have it this weekend?"

I nod, smiling. "Yeah, let's do it this weekend."

Haylie glances past my shoulder. "You will never guess who is here."

I turn to see who Haylie was talking about. Lake had walked through the door with two younger girls who looked about four. The girls were fraternal twins with matching blue denim jeans, pink jumpers with flowers decorated on them, white sneakers and their blonde hair in pigtails.

"Have you girls decided on which ice cream you're going to have?" Lake asks them.

The twins look at the different flavours, unable to make up their minds. While they tried to figure out what they wanted,

Lake glances over at Haylie and me, giving us a wave. We wave back.

"I don't trust him," Haylie tells me, making her voice low so Lake couldn't overhear us. "I mean, it's weird how he used to be rude, copying everything Gabby does. Then all of a sudden he changes, trying to be this good guy."

I nod in agreement. "I know. I wonder the same thing. Especially the night he offered to drive me to the hospital, and then act all nice about Josh."

We glanced back at Lake. The twins had finally chosen what they wanted and the clerk scoops their chosen flavours onto cones.

"You know, I don't blame him for dumping Gabby," Haylie says. "But I still don't understand why he would be interested in you."

I turn back to Haylie, not wanting Lake to think we were watching him. I scoop a spoonful of ice cream into my mouth. "I'm thinking the same thing. I mean, as soon as he found out that I liked Josh, he just started taking an interest in me. I don't know if I should take it as a good thing."

Lake pays for the ice creams and then headed over to our table with the twins, who I assumed are his sisters, behind him. "Hey, how are you guys?"

"Okay, just cheering ourselves up with ice cream," Haylie speaks for the both of us. Although I couldn't tell her that the ice cream wasn't cheering me up, having her here with me did. "So you decided not to head back to school today?" It was after one. School ends at two thirty.

Lake shakes his head. "No, I didn't see the point in going."

"True." Haylie scoops ice cream into her mouth.

"Well, I will leave you two alone. I will see you in school

tomorrow." He turns to me. "Take care of yourself, Emily. Just remember that I'm here for you if you need me."

I nod, still trying to work out why he was so desperate for me to talk to him about Josh. Haylie was the one person I wanted to talk to about him. No one else.

He smiles at me before leaving with his sisters.

"Hey, since our parents won't allow us to have a sleepover on a school night, why don't you come over for dinner instead?" Haylie asks me.

I shake my head. The offer sounded nice, but tonight I just wanted to be alone. "I don't really feel up to it tonight. But I will agree to having the sleepover this weekend."

Haylie smiles. "I look forward to it."

Chapter 19

It was freezing cold that night; somewhere down south it was snowing. As much as I hated the cold, I tried not to let it get to me as I sat on the branch of the tree in between mine and the Hopkins', resting my back against the tree trunk. Josh and I would often come out here on summer nights when it was too humid to sleep. We never came out to sit on the branch during the winter, but tonight I thought it would be nice to sit out here and think.

It was a clear night with the stars shining brightly above me, along with the moon which was full tonight. I wish Josh was here to see it.

"Emily, what are you doing out here?" I snap my gaze from the sky to where my mother was standing at my window, looking quite concerned about me sitting out here in the cold.

"I'm just gazing at the sky," I explain.

"Well, why don't you come back inside where it's warm?"

"It's okay, Mum. I don't mind sitting out here."

"Come back inside, please Emily. I don't want you to catch pneumonia."

I obey my mother just so she didn't have to worry about me. I was sure I wouldn't catch anything. I closed the window behind me, blocking out the cold air and sat down on the edge of my bed.

Mum sits down beside me. "Hey, why don't you come downstairs and be with your father and I? That way you don't have to be up here on your own. We could do something fun that can help you keep your mind off Josh."

Mum's offer sounded good, but I doubt anything will keep my mind off Josh. Everything I did remind me of him.

I give my mother a small smile. "It's okay, Mum. I'd rather stay in here."

Mum stares at me, like she was searching every part of my face to make sure I was telling the truth about being okay. It's like she knew I wasn't and that I was trying to cover everything up.

"You know, Emily, you don't have to make yourself feel like you have to lock yourself away from the world just because Josh is no longer here."

I nod. "I know. I can't help but think about him, wishing I could go back and change everything so he would still be here."

Mum gives me a small smile, pushing a strand of my hair behind my ear. "I know, sweetie. But all you can do is move forward and get through this. Josh wouldn't want you to keep thinking about him like this. You could try and distract yourself from thinking about him. Do something you love."

I shrug. "I don't know. I don't exactly feel up to doing

anything."

"Well, there is no harm in trying. It might help, Emily. Your father and I are here if you want to do something."

Mum pats my shoulder and then gets up from the bed, walking out of my room and closing the door behind her. I sit there for a moment before lying back on my bed, staring up at the ceiling. Josh was all I could think about, and I didn't know how to stop. It was easy for everyone to tell me to try and move on, but I couldn't. I just couldn't. They weren't the ones who found Josh's cold and lifeless body. It's terrifying seeing a dead body. The image was stuck in my head and I didn't know how to get rid of it.

I decided to go to bed early. At least going to sleep was the only way I could escape from thinking about him for eight hours. Only falling asleep and just forget everything was a little hard when my brain wouldn't allow me to sleep at all. Not only that, but I ended up having a dream about him. I dreamt he wasn't dead at all. It felt so real too. For a moment I thought it was real, that he wasn't dead at all and that his death was all a misunderstanding. But when I woke up in my dark room, I had to come to terms it was all a dream and Josh wasn't here.

I hate it when dreams feel real.

* * *

School is just not the place I wanted to be. I couldn't concentrate and I was tired of people looking at me with pity. Gabby was the only person who wasn't showing me pity, always acting like her nasty self. I do my best to ignore everything she says, but it wasn't easy. I tell myself not to focus on her, and to pay attention in class so I didn't fall behind. My teachers weren't going to give me a free pass into the HSC just because my best friend died.

Even when I got home later to start my homework and to catch up any work I missed yesterday, my mind was still elsewhere. I sat at my desk, wracking my brain a few times so I could focus. I had to find a way to concentrate. I thought about what my mother had said last night on how I could distract myself with something to keep Josh off my mind. I wasn't sure what to do since anything I did remind me of Josh.

Elijah and Lake wander into my mind. I recall what they had said about coming to them if I needed to talk. Haylie should be my first choice, but I wasn't ready to open up to her just yet. Maybe I should try to. Haylie was Josh's friend too, and she would be going through the same emotions as me. I shouldn't push her away. Maybe I should talk with both of the siblings. Elijah has always been a friend to Josh and I as well, even if we don't usually hang out. I can talk to him how I feel, right?

And there's Lake. I hardly talked to him at school, and it still made me wonder why he was being friendly to me. Could I even trust him with discussing how I felt? Would he keep any of it to himself without any of it going back to Gabby?

I glance at the time on my phone. 4:10pm. Haylie should be at home, baby-sitting her younger brothers, and Elijah will be at work. He won't finish until five o'clock and get home at six. Maybe I should try to talk to Lake.

Leaving my homework, I set out to take a walk around the neighbourhood. Lake lived not far from me, just four blocks away. Haylie and I walked pass his place once, where we saw him and Gabby outside his property.

Once I reach Lake's house, I stood on the sidewalk outside

his home, staring at the one-storey brick home he lived in. I hesitated about walking up to his front door and asking for him. What would Josh say about me coming here? Or even Haylie? Was Lake Terra someone I could trust?

Taking a deep breath and giving myself a quick prep talk, I made my way up to the front door. As I walk up, I half hoped that he wouldn't be home, unsure if I really wanted to be here. I knock on the front door. I hear footsteps running inside. It opens and standing there was one of the twins who was with Lake the other day at the gelato place. She stares up at me, wondering who I was. Another pair of footsteps was heard as her sister joins her.

"Who are you?" asks the second twin.

I give them a smile. "Hi. I was wondering if Lake was home?"

"Stevie, Sarah, how many times have I told you to ask who is on the other side before you open the door?" Lake comes up behind them. My heart jumps as soon as I see him, and the first thought I had was to run away. This is stupid. I shouldn't come here. Lake and I aren't even friends, even if he is trying to be friendly. I can't possibly talk to him about Josh at all.

But it was too late now. Lake was already standing at the door. "Hey, Emily."

I smile nervously. "Hi."

"Stevie, Sarah, go and see if Mum needs help in the kitchen," Lake tells his sisters.

The twins obey their brother and walk away. Lake closes the door behind him and steps out onto the veranda.

"Hey, so what brings you here?"

My stomach twists into knots. I keep telling myself I was doing the wrong thing, but I didn't know what do now that I was standing here with Lake. I couldn't arrive here and then say I had to go. That would be rude. I look into his eyes, which were deep brown, just like Josh's, and I found myself unable to turn away. His eyes reminded me of Josh so much. It felt like Josh was the one staring back at me, not Lake. All Lake had to do was dye his hair a darker shade of brown and he could look like Josh. But it's his personality that wouldn't be the same.

"I was wondering if we could hang out and talk?" I say the first thing that comes to my mind.

Lake nods. "Sure. What would you like to do? We could stay here or we could go out. Maybe we could go and get dessert or a coffee?"

"Coffee sounds good," I say even though I'm not a coffee drinker, but a hot chocolate sounded good right now. I would have decided to get dessert, but I didn't want to upset my Mum for having something before dinner. It wasn't like it matters anyway, because I still didn't have much of an appetite.

Lake disappears inside and came out shortly later with his car keys. He leads me to his car parked in the driveway, and we climb in, heading to the town centre. As he drove, I stare out of the window, unsure what I should talk to Lake about. Josh crosses my mind.

"What are you thinking about?" he asks me, catching me in my thoughts.

"Nothing," I tell him. I didn't want to tell him about my thoughts on Josh. If I did, he will probably ask me questions about him I didn't want to answer.

We stay silent for the rest of the ride. Once in town, we stop at a café where he got himself a latte and I ordered myself a hot chocolate. We sit at one of the tables.

"So how are you coping?" Lake asks me, taking a sip of his

latte.

I sip my drink before I answer. "I still feel the same way since I found Josh. I can't sleep or eat. I don't want to do anything. Last night my mum told me to try and distract myself with something that could help me get Josh off my mind."

"Have you found something to help you get him off your mind?"

I sit there, my hands around my cup as I let it warm them. I haven't thought of him since we had reached the café, and now he had found his way back into my mind again. Maybe if Lake hadn't mention him, maybe just for a little while I could have successfully gotten him off my mind.

In that moment, memories of Josh flashes through my mind. The first memory I see is when Josh and I share our first kiss. I saw him smiling. I saw him laughing. Those memories were all I had of him.

"Emily?"

I look up when I hear Josh's voice calling my name. There, sitting beside me is Josh. I blink a few times to make sure what I was seeing is real. I no longer cared that Lake was the one who was meant to be sitting next to me in this café.

But when I hear my name being called again, Josh disappears and is replace by Lake. He sits there, concern written on his face. It almost made me feel bad that he was sitting here, being concerned about me while I just wished he would turn back into Josh.

I wanted Josh. I wanted to see his face. I wanted to hold him, and to have him tell me that this is all a dream. That he isn't dead.

Lake reaches across the table and takes my hand in his. With his other hand, he rests it under my chin and makes me look at him. "Hey, it's okay, Emily. Everything will be fine. You will get through this."

But I don't want to move on and forget about him, I wanted to say. *I just want him here with me.*

"No, Lake," my voice coming out aggressive more than I meant it to. When was everyone going to stop saying everything is fine? "Nothing is going to be fine. It never will be. Josh is dead and I don't know how I'm supposed to move on."

Lake opens his mouth slightly to say something, but then he closes it. Instead, he pushes a strand of my hair away from my face and leans towards me. As soon as he does, I immediately think back to when Josh and I kissed.

What the hell is Lake doing?

I push him away before he could brush his lips against mine, not wanting to make a scene. "Lake," I growl.

He gets the message. "Sorry. I didn't mean to upset you."

Shaking my head, I get up from the table, taking my cup with me. "I'm sorry. I thought I could come out here and hang out with you, hoping I could distract myself for a moment, but I don't think I can do it."

I hurry out of the café and down the street. I have to get as far away from Lake.

But that wasn't going to be easy.

He catches up to me down the street, grabs my arm to stop me from running off and spins me around to face him.

"Emily, stop," he begs, his eyes full of concern. "I'm sorry for back there. But I want you to know that you can do this. Don't think you can't distract yourself for a moment. Why don't we go catch a movie?"

I shake my head. "Thanks, Lake, but I think I'm just going to go home. Thank you for coming out here with me."

Lake nods, stroking my face. "Emily, come on. You don't

have to leave so soon."

I push his hand away. I didn't want his sympathy or for him to comfort me. His sympathy was making me think of Josh even more. If I'm going to move on from Josh's death, I need to be alone to mourn.

"I need to go, Lake."

Before I could turn to walk away, Lake leans over to try and kiss me for the second time.

I shove him back, frowning. "No, Lake. I'm not interested."

Lake looks at me confused. "What do you mean you aren't interested? I thought you wanted to hang out."

"Yeah, as friends, Lake. I'm sorry, but I'm not interested in you. I'm not interested in anyone. The one person I want to be with is no longer here."

I walk away before Lake could stop me. He calls out to me as I come to the kerb. I look both ways before crossing, not daring to look back at Lake.

I reach a park and sit down on a bench, pulling out my phone to call Haylie. She answers and I ask her if she could come pick me up. I could walk home, but it was an hour and a half to my place. I could call one of my parents to come get me, but I didn't really feel like talking to them about what had happened and what I was doing in the town centre. I never told them where I was going, except just for a walk.

"Sure, I will be there soon, Emily," she says.

I force myself to smile. "Thanks, Haylie."

She must have detected a hint of sadness in my voice. "Is everything okay, Em?"

I nod even though she can't see me. I didn't tell her about Lake. "I'm fine."

She doesn't push for questions. "Okay. I will be there soon."

Chapter 20

"I can't believe that jerk tried to kiss you," Haylie says as she drives me home. I had told her what had happened between Lake and me. "Doesn't he know what you're going through?"

"I don't know what made him think I was interested in him," I say. "I have told him once that I just wanted to hang out as friends. All I wanted to do this afternoon was distract myself from thinking about Josh, like my mum had suggested for me to do. So I thought I would take Lake's offer of hanging out. Only I fell apart instead. Lake's eyes reminded me of Josh's, and then he asked how I was coping with his death. I think I fell apart more when he tried to kiss me. It made me think of when Josh and I kissed on Saturday night right before he ended his life."

I leave out the part where I had briefly heard Josh's voice and when I had seen him in Lake's place at the table. Haylie doesn't need to know about that.

Haylie turns to me with a smile. "You know, you never really talked to me about that kiss." She turns back to the road. "I know with everything, you never wanted to talk about it. But if you want to, I would love to hear about it. What was it like kissing Josh? Who made the first move?"

I replay the kiss in my mind. Josh cupping his hands around my jaw. He moves slowly towards me while I meet him half way, closing my eyes as I press my lips against his.

Oh, how I wish I could feel Josh's lips against mine again.

I bite my lip, not wanting to cry. I can't discuss this with Haylie right now.

"I know you want to know everything about it, and I will tell you," I tell Haylie. "But right now, I just can't bear to think about it."

Haylie nods. "I understand. Take all the time you need, Emily. And try not to worry too much about Lake. If he doesn't understand or respect what you're feeling, then he isn't worth it."

"Enough about me. How are you and Jensen? Sorry if I never asked you with everything that has been going on."

"No need to apologise," Haylie says with a smile. "Everything is going good between us. We haven't kissed yet. The date we went on when you and Josh went camping went very well. We are planning to go out again this Friday."

I smile at my friend. "That's great, Haylie. I'm glad everything is working out well with Jensen."

Haylie pulls up in front of my house, parking behind a blue Ford Focus hatchback that's parked on the street. I say goodbye and thanked her for coming to pick me up. I tell her I will see her tomorrow.

Once inside the house, I find my parents in the lounge room. They were grinning about something.

"Hey, Emily," Mum greets me. "Did you have a nice walk?"

I nod. "I did. I met up with Haylie and she drove me back home." I leave out Lake. I don't feel like discussing him with my parents.

"That's good to hear. So, what do you think, Emily?"

I stare at my parents with a puzzled look. "What do I think of what?"

"Did you see the blue Ford Focus out front?" Dad asks.

"I have. What about it?"

"It's your new car."

A wide smile breaks out across my lips. I was not expecting a new car, especially after passing my driver's test almost two weeks ago. My parents and I never even discussed what kind of car I should get. But I guess with everything that has been happening, maybe my parents just wanted to surprise me with it and cheer me up.

"Are you serious?" I squeal.

Dad stands up, grabbing the keys from the coffee table. He hands them to me with a smile. "Seriously. Your mother and I put some money together. We are both very proud of you for passing your test."

I look at the keys in my hands and then glance at my parents. "Thank you so much. I really wasn't expecting you to get me a car."

Dad pats my shoulder. "We have been saving for a while and planned to get your first car once you had pass. Enjoy it, Em."

"But maybe take the car for spin tomorrow afternoon after school," Mum says. "It's getting dark and I have dinner ready."

"I'm not hungry," I tell her.

Mum gives me a concerned look. "Emily, you need to eat something. Just have a little bit of food."

I agreed even though all I wanted was to escape to my room.

* * *

Haylie waits for me at the front of the school the next morning, and I excitedly tell her about the car my parents had gotten me. She squeals, suggesting we go for a drive after school to celebrate this milestone. It was an excellent idea, but I decided I wanted to go for a drive myself. To be alone with my own thoughts.

The school day seemed to dragged and all I wanted was for it to be over. I ignore Lake the best I could. He made an attempt to talk to me, to apologise for yesterday, but Gabby then calls him over and tells him not to talk to losers like me. Still listening to Gabby, I see.

Letting my thoughts drift off during my classes, I thought of the one place I wanted to visit.

As soon as school finishes for the day, I drive to Deighton Falls Campgrounds. It may not be the best place to be, but I want to be here. I want to think and be alone.

My stomach twists into knots as I approach the campgrounds, replaying back the memories of that weekend. I don't know how I'm going to react once I reach here. I tell myself that it isn't too late to turn around, that maybe it's too soon to come back here.

I pull into the parking lot. It was almost four thirty and it will soon be sunset. No one was camping that afternoon, but there were a few cars in the car park where people were probably walking the trails.

Getting out of the car, I glance around the campground. There's a chill in the air and it wasn't from the cold. Taking a deep breath, I give myself a quick prep talk. *I can do this. I need to do it.*

I walk around to the camp site Josh and I had set camp at. I stand there for a moment, lost in thoughts about the night. I replay back in my head so many times, wondering what had gone wrong that night. What made Josh think that he shouldn't keep living anymore? Didn't he care how I would feel or what anyone would feel about his actions?

But of course, the reason why he left was because of me. He didn't want to hurt me. I shouldn't have told him how I felt towards him. I shouldn't have let him kiss me. I wish I could tell Josh that he wasn't hurting me, that I didn't care about his illness. I never judged him for it. I was always there for him as he came to terms with schizophrenia. Why would he think I deserved someone better than him? I didn't want anyone else but Josh.

I try to think like Josh, try to be in his shoes of that night, but I just couldn't understand what he must have been thinking. I still wanted to kick myself for not waking up. If I had woken up, I could have stopped Josh.

I leave the camp site, walking to the trail leading to the lookout. A lump in my throat forms as I walk it, not knowing how I'm going to react once I get to the lookout. I bite my lip, fighting back the tears that are threatening to fall.

When I do reach it, I stand near the trees, afraid to walk any further to the platform. I close my eyes and tell myself I can do this. I can be brave.

I hear voices nearby. I open my eyes to see a group of people heading my way from where they had come back up to where they had come from the waterfall. I move towards the lookout as they walk pass me.

I stand at the railing, looking out at the waterfall. I don't dare to glance down at where I found Josh's body. I pull out my phone, tapping on my photo gallery and glance at the last photo I had taken of Josh and me. We'd posed together at the lookout. He was happy there. How did everything change in an instant that night? Did his hallucinations say something to him? Georgia, I know, would encourage him not to do any of this. She was sweet, and would have told him how lucky he was to have someone like me who could understand him. Aspen, the jerk, would probably have said something negative, but wouldn't encourage him to do something to threaten his life. Even Davis wouldn't. His other hallucinations he doesn't tell me about probably wouldn't. At least I don't think so. Georgia, Aspen and Davis always looked out for Josh. They always made sure he was taking care of himself, that he was getting the right amount of sleep or that he was eating. There were days when they encouraged him to take his medication, but there were also days when they might tell him the medication is no good and he doesn't need it. The voices in his head, on the other hand, are always negative, telling him how he is no good and how he ruins people's lives. I wish I knew what they had said to him about me. If I could hear those voices, I would tell them to go away and to stop twisting Josh's head with lies. If I could see Georgia, Aspen, Davis and his other hallucinations, I would have told them to stop Josh from jumping.

Biting my lip, I put my phone away.

I wish I could go back and change everything.

I want Josh here with me. Nothing will ever be the same

without him.

"Smile, Emily," I hear Josh's voice in my head. "Don't look so down."

"It's hard to smile when you aren't here, Josh," I answer out loud.

"What do you mean, Em? I'm right here."

It then occurs to me that I wasn't hearing Josh's voice in my head. He sounded nearby. When I turn to my left, there is Josh standing beside me in the last thing I remember seeing him in – jeans, black t-shirt and a blue hoodie. I blink a few times, making sure I wasn't seeing things. This couldn't be real, but here is Josh, standing right before me. How was that possible when he was dead? He has to be a hallucination.

But I'm not going crazy, am I?

I think back to yesterday when I heard Josh calling my name in the café, and him sitting where Lake was. Was he real? Or was my head playing with me, making me think he was real when he wasn't?

"Josh?"

He smiles. "Hi, Emily."

"How are you here, Josh? You died."

Josh has to be a hallucination. Or maybe I can secretly see dead people. Except Josh is the *only* dead person I could see.

"Go away, Josh," I say. "You aren't real."

"If I wasn't real, I wouldn't be talking to you."

"Your hallucinations aren't real, and you interact with them all the time. You may not talk to them when I am around, but you probably spoke to them when I'm not there."

I turn away from him, looking out at the waterfall. If I ignore him, he will go away.

But that isn't what he does. He steps closer to me, putting

his hand over mine. I look down at his hand. His palm feels warm over mine. I force myself to look at him, his brown eyes staring back at me. I wanted to believe that he wasn't dead, that he wasn't a hallucination or a ghost. But right now, I don't understand what I'm seeing. Are my eyes playing tricks on me? Or is my brain doing this?

No, no, no. I can't be losing my insanity right now. I just can't. Josh is dead. He isn't standing right here beside me. He's a hallucination. A ghost.

My heart races in my chest, and I find myself unable to breathe. No, I can't be insane.

I move my hand away from Josh, turning my back to him.

"Emily?" he asks me. "What's wrong? Are you okay?"

I squeeze my eyes shut and ran my hands through my hair, pulling hard on the roots.

I'm not crazy, I'm not crazy.

"You aren't real," I tell him. "You aren't here. You're gone."

Josh is beside me, making me turn to him and pulling my arms down. "Emily, breathe. I need you to calm down."

I listen, inhaling deep breaths and exhaling them.

"Now, open your eyes."

I shake my head.

"Emily, open your eyes."

"No. I'm not opening them. I refuse to believe I'm going crazy. I shouldn't be seeing you and I shouldn't be talking to you. You aren't real. You died, Josh. I saw your body when you died. You aren't here. Please don't make me open my eyes."

Josh strokes my cheek. "Don't be scared to open them. I know this is a shock to you, but I promise everything is okay."

I listen to Josh and slowly open my eyes. He stands there, concern in his eyes. We stare at each other for a long time before I reach up to touch his face, tracing my fingers along his jaw, his nose, mouth, then down his neck, shoulders and down his arms. He felt real enough. He has to be a hallucination, not a ghost. I don't think I could feel him if he was a spirit. But I don't understand how I'm seeing him. I have never had a hallucination. So why was I having it now?

I stand back from Josh, looking him up and down. "I don't understand. How am I seeing you?"

Josh shrugs. "I don't know. Our brains do weird stuff sometimes."

I'm sure there was some kind of explanation to why I was seeing Josh right here. Or when I heard and saw him in the café yesterday.

Whatever was going on with me, I was just glad to see Josh.

I hug him tightly and he wraps his arms around me. The tears are overtaking me now as I sob in his chest. "I'm so glad to see you, Josh. I have missed you so much."

Josh pulls away from me and wipes my tears. "I have missed you too. I'm so sorry about everything, Emily."

"Why did you leave, Josh?"

He turns away. "I had to. I was hurting you."

I shake my head, making him look at me. I think back to the letter he had written me. "No, you weren't. I loved you, Josh. You were my best friend. If I felt like I was hurt by you, or if I didn't want to be around you because of your illness, I would have left as soon as you were diagnosed. But I stayed because you were my friend. I helped you get through everything. And I never felt like you were a burden, Josh, because you weren't."

Josh looks at me with sadness. "I'm sorry I did this to you, Emily. Not just to you, but to everyone. It's just… this illness sometimes takes over me. I fight so hard every day to ignore the voices in my head that tell me I'm no good. Even with medication, they are still there, telling me what I should be doing. I'm sorry, Emily."

I rest my hand on Josh's cheek and he leans into it. "That night when you kissed me, what did the voices say? What did Georgia and the others say?"

"Georgia was thrilled that we had kissed. Even when Aspen tells me stupid stuff, he was happy for me. Davis wasn't there when we kissed. And the voices…" He turns away from me. "The voices told me that you were lying and that you didn't love me. I'm ruining your life by being with you. And then this overpowering voice said I should do you a favour and disappear, that's what you would want me to do… I wish I didn't let the voices control me. Davis was there with me on the lookout. He told me to think about you, to get out of here while I could so he could protect me. Someone was coming for me. I don't know what it was. I believed Davis when he said he will protect me, but I panicked when they came for me, threatening me with these negative things. I panicked, didn't know what to do. I wanted to go back to you, but I was afraid of what would happen if I had gone back to you. Would they had come for you to hurt me? And before I could change my mind about anything, to protect you, I slipped and that was it."

There's a brief silence between us as I begin to understand what Josh did, that the words in his letter were the things the voices had told him to write. He didn't want to jump. He felt like he needed to at first, but then Davis convinced him to go back to me. That's what Josh was going to do, afraid whatever was after him will come for me, but he panicked as he tried to get back over the railing and slipped.

"I'm sorry, Emily," he softly says. "Please forgive me."

I do. I cup my hands around his jaw and kiss him. His lips against mine felt exactly how it had that night when we kissed for the first time. I wanted to go back to that night. I wanted to change everything. I wanted to tell him that everything will be okay, that he was safe, that I was safe.

Whether my brain was playing tricks on me and Josh wasn't really here, I didn't care. All that matters that he was here with me right now. I could touch him. I could see him. I want him here with me.

* * *

We stay at Deighton Falls for a little while longer before heading back home. Josh came with me. I put on the heater, and we sang along with the radio, having the time of our lives. It felt good to have him back.

I parked the car on the street. I look towards the house before I got out. It was now dark and the lights were on inside.

I turn to Josh. "I have to keep you a secret, okay, Josh? I don't want anyone to know I'm talking to you. I don't want anyone to think I'm crazy."

He nods. "I completely understand, Emily."

I smile at him, and then we get out of the car, walking up the front lawn, hand-in-hand.

"Emily, is that you?" I hear my mother call from the kitchen once I had reached inside.

"Yes," I call back.

Mum appears in the doorway of the kitchen, smiling. "How was the drive? And most importantly, how is the car?"

I smile brightly. "The car was great, and so was the drive."

"Where did you go?"

"I drove up to Deighton Falls."

She looks at me with concern. "How did it go up there?"

"I'm okay, Mum, if that's what you're asking. I just felt like it was the place I needed to go to for closure."

Mum gives me a small smile. "Did you get any closure?"

I chew the inside of my cheek. "I think so."

"That's good, sweetie. Dinner is on the table. Your father and I have already eaten."

"I will eat something in a moment. I'm just going to go up to my room."

Before Mum could say anything to me, I turn and walk up the stairs, still holding onto Josh's hand. Once in my room, I close the door, switching on the light. Josh walks straight over to the window, glancing across to his room. The light was on in there where I saw Lynn packing away his belongings into cardboard boxes. My heart crumbles in my chest when I see her. She shouldn't have to be packing away any of Josh's belongings.

"How are Phillip and Lynn?" Josh asks me.

I join him at the window, closing the blinds so Lynn couldn't snoop in and see me talking to Josh.

"Okay, I guess," I answer him. "Everyone is still shock with what you had done."

He turns to me. "I wish I could go back and change everything."

I nod. "Same here, Josh."

But what's done is done. Nothing could bring Josh back now.

A knock came from the door, follow by my mother's voice. "Emily, Lake is at the door. He wants to speak with you."

I turn from Josh in the direction of the door. "Okay. Tell him I will be down in a sec."

I turn back to Josh, seeing the confusion on his face.

"Why is Lake here?"

"Lake has been coming around checking up on me to make sure I'm coping okay."

"Since when does he do that? I thought he wasn't allowed to talk to you because Gabby tells him not to."

"Well, now that he isn't dating her, he has been talking to me." I stroke his cheek. "Don't worry, Josh. I'm being careful around him." I peck his lips and then head out of my room.

I close the front door and step out on the veranda. "What can I do for you, Lake?"

"I wanted to apologise for my behaviour yesterday," he says. "I wanted to say something at school today, but you made it pretty clear that you didn't want me to come anywhere near you. So I hope you don't mind that I have come here. I was a dick yesterday, and I realise that I shouldn't have tried to kiss you. Not without your permission. If you forgive me, I would like to make it up to you by taking you out for dinner tomorrow night."

I stare at him, wondering when he was going to get the message that I wasn't interested in him. What part of being 'just friends' did he not understand?

"I forgive you, Lake," I say. "Thanks, but I told you that I'm only interested in being friends. But it's clear you don't want to be just friends. I can't be with you, Lake. I hope you understand that."

I head back inside before he could say anything else.

Josh was lying on my bed when I walked in. I lie down beside him.

"What did Lake want?" he asks.

"He asked me out, but I said no. I'm not interested in being with him or anyone right now."

Josh smiles, taking my hand into his.

We talk like old times until we eventually fall asleep side by side.

Chapter 21

Josh isn't there when I wake up in the morning, and a wave of sadness hits me hard. Yesterday afternoon was the happiest I have ever been after everything that happened this past week. Not seeing Josh in my room that morning hit me hard, reminding me he was still gone and seeing him yesterday was all in my head. I wonder if he will appear later when I at least expect him to.

I didn't mention to Haylie about Josh when I arrive at school. I didn't want her to think I was crazy, even though I'm sure she would listen to me if I told her what was happening. I also didn't want her to worry that something could be wrong with me, because I know there isn't. I look around for Josh, hoping I would see him around school, but he wasn't there. And I began to wonder if seeing him was just a once off thing.

Haylie looks at me as we walk to maths, her brows furrowed.

"Are you okay, Emily?"

My face flushes at the question, like I've been caught doing something I shouldn't. "Of course I'm okay. Why wouldn't I be?"

"You seem distracted, that's all. I have been talking to you about the maths homework we were meant to do last night, but you don't seem to be listening to a word I have been saying. You keep looking everywhere. Are you looking for someone or something?"

I don't look at her, afraid she would see right through me. How do I explain to her that I'm trying to find someone who isn't even supposed to exist?

"Ah, no," I answer. "I'm not looking for anyone. Sorry. I just have a lot on my mind."

"Anything you want to talk about? Josh?"

I saw Josh yesterday, I wanted to say to her. *I talked to him. I touched him. It seems crazy, but he felt so real, like he wasn't even gone. He told me everything that happened that night. And that suicide note he left me, that wasn't even him that wrote it. It was the voices telling him to do it. He was going to jump, but Davis convinced him not to. He was going to come back to me, protect me from whatever was coming after him, but he slipped and fell.*

The words were on the edge of my tongue, dying to tell Haylie everything. But I couldn't tell her any of it without sounding like I have lost my mind.

"I'm fine," I tell her.

No, you aren't fine, I tell myself.

"You will tell me if something isn't fine, will you?"

I hesitate on answering, pressing my lips into a thin line. "Of course."

Liar!

We take our normal seat in the back row of the classroom. We barely had the chance to take out our stuff before Lake strolls in, making his way over to us.

"Hey," he says to me with a smile. "How are you doing?"

Why can't he just leave me alone already?

But I don't tell him this as much as I like to. Instead I return the smile, and say, "I'm good."

"Lake, get over here and stop talking to Mrs Freak," Gabby says from across the room. She takes a seat in the middle row on the left side of the classroom.

Lake doesn't move straight away, still watching me and then turns, walking over to Gabby.

"Well, I guess it shows that he still listens to his bitchy ex-girlfriend, even though he said he wants nothing to do with her," Haylie says in a low whisper that only I can hear.

Mr Carlson walks into the room, greeting us all. He tells us what page of the textbook to turn to, continuing on the topic of algebra.

Rather than paying attention to my teacher, I turn to look at Josh's desk. For a moment I was hoping he would appear and he will be sitting at his desk. But of course, last night was just a stupid hallucination. Josh wasn't going to reappear. Last night was just a one-off thing, like some kind of closure. And the thought of it made me feel lonely inside.

Something hit my head. When I turn, I see a scrunch up paper had hit my head, and was now in front of me on the table. As soon as I saw it, I knew it was from Gabby. I glance over at her. She was looking my way, a big smirk on her face. I turn to my teacher, making sure he wasn't looking my way. Thankfully Mr Carlson had his back to the class as he wrote out equations on the board, and hadn't taken any notice of Gabby throwing things at me. Of course he didn't. He never takes any notice of what she does.

I unfold the ball of paper, smoothing it out on the table to see what that bitch had written. Haylie leans in to read the note also.

Stop staring at Freak's desk. He isn't here anymore, and staring at it won't make him come back. Forget about him. By the way, he doesn't love you. If he did, he wouldn't have killed himself.

I bite my lip as tears fill my eyes and my heart stabs itself. How could someone so cold-hearted like Gabrielle Casey say those words? How would she feel if she was in my position? Would she still be saying those things she was saying in her note? Would she even stay friends with them if they were diagnosed with a mental illness, or would she had ditch them a long time ago as soon as they showed signs of an illness before they even had the chance to get help?

And how could she say Josh didn't love me? How would she know what he had or hadn't? Josh didn't end his life. He told me he wasn't. He told me he wrote the letter to me because that's what the voices were telling him to do. He stood on the ledge not because he wanted to, but the voices told him to. And when he decided to go back to me, he had slipped. But, of course, no one was going to see it as that. They will see it as suicide.

No one will never know what was going through Josh's head.

Haylie pats my shoulder and whispers, "Don't listen to her, Emily." Her whisper sounded like Josh, telling me everything was going to be okay. "She doesn't know what she is talking about."

I don't respond to her. A mixture of anger and sadness rises within me. Taking slow deep breaths to stop myself from losing it doesn't help. I tell myself to let go of Gabby's words and not let them get to me, but it was so hard to ignore them when they really hit you where it hurts. I knew the things she was saying was untrue. She just wanted to make me feel bad.

I wanted to repeat everything to her about what Josh had said to me last night, about what he was going to do and how he was going to come back to me. Davis had tried to help him. He knew what the voices in his head were doing, and he was trying to help Josh to fight it. He promised Josh he would protect him, and to go back to me.

But he slipped! He slipped and fell!

I should have been there. I should have woken up and followed him. I should have been at the railing with him. That way when he had slipped, I could have helped him. I could have saved Josh.

I have to go. I have to get out of here.

I gather up my stuff. Haylie watches me, wondering what I was doing. I then stood up from my desk, my chair scraping against the carpet. The noise catches the attention of my classmates as they turn to me, including Mr Carlson.

He turns from the whiteboard, frowning. "What are you doing, Miss Carter? Sit back down."

I ignore him, running out the door before anyone could see the tears in my eyes. I ran down the empty corridors, heading towards the girls' bathroom.

The bathroom was empty. I hid myself inside a stall and lock the door. I sat down on the tile floor, curling up into a ball and buried my face in my knees, hugging my legs.

A pair of arms wraps around me into a hug, and then the

person whispers into my ear, "It's going to be alright."

The anger and sadness subside once I hear Josh's voice. Wiping my eyes and turn to him where he sat beside me. I smile at him. "You're back."

"Who said I had gone anywhere?"

"I was worried you had left."

He strokes my face. "I'm not going anywhere, Emily."

"I don't understand how Gabby can be so cruel. She doesn't even care how I feel. It hurt when she said you didn't love me. If you had loved me, you wouldn't have ended your life. I know what she said wasn't true. You do love me."

Josh rubs a hand up and down my arm. "Don't listen to her. Gabby doesn't know what she is talking about. And yes, I do love you."

I cross my legs at my ankles. "Why is it hard to move on? I don't exactly want to move on."

Josh rocks me gently in his arms. "I don't know. I guess that's part of grieving. Everyone goes through a different way of grieving. It was hard to move on after my parents passed away. I keep wondering each day that what if we hadn't gotten into the car. What if we had stayed at home instead? When the doctor informed me that my parents didn't make it, I didn't talk to anyone for months. No one understood what I had went through. They can only imagine what I had gone through. It was hard to move on."

I take in a shaky breath. "I keep seeing the image of you on the rocks when I looked over the cliff. I have never seen a dead body before. How do I move on from what I have seen? How do I just get that image out of my head?"

Josh strokes my face gently. "Hey, you move on when you're ready. And if no one can understand how you feel, then at least we have each other. I will help you get through this, Emily."

"How Josh? You aren't exactly real. You are a hallucination."

"Maybe I am, but I can be as real as you want me to be. I am here for you."

I smile. "Thanks, Josh."

He returns the smile, and pushes some of my hair away from my face that managed to escape my ponytail. He leans over to kiss me just as the door to the restroom swings open. We jump apart and remain quiet so the person couldn't hear us talking. I didn't want them to hear what we were talking about, or to think I was crazy for talking to myself.

"Emily, are you in here?" Haylie's voice echoes through the room.

Great, Haylie is here. I hope she hadn't heard Josh and me talking.

Instead of getting up to show my face, I stay where I was on the tile floor. Josh has a hand on my shoulder. "Yeah, I'm in here."

Haylie walks over to the stall and lay down on her stomach, peaking under the door. "Are you okay?"

I give her a small smile. "I'm okay. Sorry I ran out of the classroom like that."

"It's no problem. But I'm probably not the person you should apologise to. Mr Carlson is the one you should apologise to."

"I know. I just need a few minutes to myself after what Gabby wrote."

"Do you think you are ready to come back? Mr Carlson is extremely furious with you for walking out of the class."

I turn to Josh and whisper. "I will see you later."

He smiles.

I get up from the floor and leave the stall, giving Haylie a hug. Together we walk back to class. As soon as I return, Mr Carlson has me stay out in the corridor, where he scolds me. I explain to him why I had run out of the classroom. I thought he would give me a detention, but he decides to let me off with a warning. I thank him, and sit back down with Haylie, ignoring the stares I get from my classmates. I keep my eyes on my work and the teacher, refusing to look at Gabby, who I know would be giving me a smirk.

Chapter 22

I never told my parents what was going on at school, how Gabrielle Casey wasn't a nice person and the things she would say about me or Josh. I figured I would cause too much trouble if I say anything. They would want to talk to Mr Mathison about what was going on, and I didn't want to cause any trouble. Gabby will make my life even more miserable than she already does.

That night my parents went out for their nineteenth wedding anniversary. They left me with some money and I order pizza. It was cool outside, but I decided I wanted to catch the last remainder of the sun, and sat out on the patio with the pizza. The sky was a shade of pink and orange.

Josh appears, grabbing a slice of pizza. "I haven't had pizza for so long." He bites into the Hawaiian pizza, and then talks with his mouth full. "I don't even remember the last time I ate it."

"I think it has been a while since I had pizza too," I say.

"This pizza tastes so good." He moans as he chews his food.

We eat our food in silence. It was nice to have Josh as company. A thought then drifts into my mind.

"Josh, do you ever wonder what it would be like if you hadn't died?" I ask him.

It's a question I keep wondering to myself. Like would we be a couple now? Where will we both be once we graduate high school next month?

Josh sits there in silence as he finishes chewing the rest of his pizza, taking time to process my question. "Sometimes I found it hard to think positive and what the future could hold for me. But when I did think about it, I always thought about what could happen if you and I were more than friends. That night we kissed, I swear it was the happiest day of my life. I used to think that you didn't share the same feelings as me, so I was always afraid to tell you how I felt." He closes his eyes, shaking his head. "I feel so damn stupid for listening to that voice, telling me you will never love me and that I'm better off killing myself." He opens his eyes, forcing himself to look at me. "I should have ignored it. Davis did what he did to stop me so I could go back to you, but I slipped."

I smile at him, reaching across the table and taking his hand into mine. Our fingers intertwine with each other.

"Emily, is everything alright?" Lynn's voice comes from next door.

I jump at the sound of her voice, letting go of Josh's hand. I glance over at my neighbour's yard and see Lynn peeking over the fence. I wasn't even aware that she was outside, and I knew she must have heard my conversation with Josh. What will she think about me talking to him? Will she tell my parents?

"Yes, everything is alright, Lynn." I give her a small smile.

She looks at me, unsure she wanted to believe me. "Okay, well you have a good night."

"You too, Lynn."

Lynn disappears and I hear her walking back inside.

I turn to Josh. "We should get back inside. It's not safe to talk out here."

I couldn't risk being caught talking to him. Lynn would be sure to tell my parents what's going on, and I didn't want them to think there was something wrong with me for talking to someone who wasn't there. I mean, there isn't anything wrong with me, is there? I don't know the reason why I'm seeing Josh, but I know I'm not going crazy...

I think.

We clean up the mess and head indoors just as someone knocked on the door. I wasn't expecting anyone tonight. Haylie had offered to come over this evening when I told her it was my parents' anniversary, but I told her I wanted to be alone. I feel bad telling her I wanted to be alone every time she asks for us to hang out. I know she was looking out for me, and I appreciate it. I just need this time with myself to figure out things.

Leaving Josh in the kitchen, I went to answer it. Standing there was Lake. He was the last person I was expecting to see. He has already apologised to me. Why does he keep coming around and trying to talk to me? Why doesn't he get the message that I'm not interested in him?

"Lake, hey."

"Hey, I hope I'm not interrupting anything."

I shake my head. "No, you're not. What can I do for you, Lake?"

"I just wanted to come by and see you how you are after what Gabby did today. I wanted to ask you at school, but I couldn't find you after maths. I also didn't want Gabby to see me talking to you."

Again, he is letting her control him. He should be allowed to talk to whoever he wants.

"That's nice of you to come by, but you really don't need to come and check on me every time Gabby does something nasty. I'm fine. Really." I give him a small smile.

"I know." He looks down at his feet. "I also stop by because I wanted to see you again." He looks up to see how I would react.

I stare at him, unsure whether I should just slam the door in Lake's face and go back inside to be with Josh. But at the same time, I didn't want to be rude. I just want Lake to realise that I'm not interested, and that I clearly do not see us being friends or being more than that. I don't even think we would be good as friends either. We are too different, and if he is someone who hangs out with Gabrielle Casey than I don't want to have anything to do with him. And even though he has not mention it, but I'm pretty sure he is just saying he likes me to make Gabby jealous, and I didn't want to be part of that.

"Are you back with Gabby again?" It was the first thing that came to my head, especially when I'm pretty sure he had told me he didn't want anything to do with her. Yet today she told him to stay away from me and to sit with her.

"We still talk. She's in my friend group."

I glance over my shoulder, hoping Josh doesn't appear.

"Well, thanks for stopping by, Lake," I say. "I will see you in school tomorrow."

I start to close the door when Lake stops me from closing it.

"Wait. Would it be okay if I get a glass of water before I go?"

No, I want you to leave so I can be alone, I wanted to say.

I nod, and move aside so he could come in. He stands there in the foyer, looking around. I close the door and lead him to the kitchen. I avoid contact with Josh, knowing what he will say when he sees Lake. I grab a glass from the cabinet and fill it with water. I turn to him, where he was standing at the kitchen island, and hand him the glass. Lake thanks me, taking a long gulp.

I lean back on the counter as Josh walks over and stands beside me, whispering even though only I could hear him, "What is he doing here, Emily?"

"It's okay, Josh," I whisper back. "He only came here to see how I was after what happened at school today. He will leave as soon as he finishes his drink."

Josh looks at me, his eyes filled with worry. "What if he doesn't leave, Em?"

"He will, Josh. Don't worry too much."

"Who are you talking to?" Lake asks me, putting his glass down on the counter.

I turn to face Lake. He gives me this strange look like I was some kind of weirdo as I talked to myself.

I quickly came up with an excuse so I didn't sound like some crazy person. "Uh, no one. Sorry. I was just thinking out loud."

That should be a good enough excuse, right?

Lake doesn't say anything. He just nods. I think he brought my lie.

He then steps forward. My heart pounds when he cups his hands around my face. He kisses me before I had the chance to stop him. I push him off me as soon his lips touched mine. We stare at each other. I narrow my eyes at him. Before I had the chance to give him a piece of my mind, he moves to kiss me again. This time I didn't allow his lips to touch mine. I slap him across the face.

He covers his face where I had slapped him, rubbing it. "Ow, you bitch! Why the hell did you do that for, Emily?"

I frown at him. Did he really not know why I'd slapped him?

"You're seriously asking me that question? Why do you think I did it? You kissed me without my consent, you jerk! I thought I had made it clear that I only want to be friends. That's it. Nothing else. I'm in love with Josh."

Lake snickers. "Wow. You're in love with a dead person."

The way he says it crushes my heart.

I look over at Josh standing beside me, and he stares right back at me, concerned, worried about what Lake is going to do. He clenches his fist at his side, glancing at Lake. He takes a step forward and gets ready to swing.

"No, don't!" I raise my voice at Josh.

Josh turns to me. "I'm not letting him get away with this."

"Who are you talking to?" Lake asks me, giving me another weird look.

I realise how ridiculous I look. Why oh why is he here? If Lake hadn't shown up, it will just be Josh and me alone in this house. I can't imagine what he is thinking or the things he is going to say to Gabby and others at school if I am talking to myself.

"No one."

"No one?" Lake chuckles. "You know something? Gabby is right about you. You spend way too much time with Freak. Keep talking to yourself and you will become exactly like him."

My heart crushes in my chest when Lake said that, especially calling Josh a freak. He had promised me he was never going to call him that. I was happy when he was finally calling him by his proper name. But I guess it doesn't matter what I say because Gabby has him wrapped around her finger. Anything she says, he does.

I give him a filthy look. "Don't call Josh that ever again. And I'm not becoming Josh. Talking to myself doesn't make me crazy. You know, I really don't understand why you have been trying to act all nice to me. I thought you would have least respect me when I said I just want to be friends. But clearly you don't seem to care about that. It's all about what you want. Not what I want."

Lake snickers. "Whatever. At least I'm not talking to someone who isn't here."

The way he says it sends a shiver down my spine. I'm still not understanding why I'm able to see Josh, and there is no way I could tell Lake he was here. He would definitely have me locked away.

"You need to leave," I tell him.

"My pleasure. I don't want to be in the same room as some crazy person who talks to themselves."

Without another word, Lake walks out of the kitchen and out the front door. Good. He was gone. But even though he was gone, I was worried he might tell someone I was acting weird, especially to Gabby. I don't want to know what she will say or do if she knew I was talking to myself. No one will ever believe me that Josh was here with me.

Tears fill my eyes, but I quickly wipe them away.

Josh pats my shoulder.

I don't look at him. "Josh, do you think Lake will tell someone I was talking to you?"

Josh twirls me around so I was facing him. "Even if he does, he can't prove you are." He strokes my cheek. "Don't worry about it too much, okay?"

I smile. "Okay."

I kiss him, wrapping my arms around his neck. I was glad Josh was here with me.

Chapter 23

My parents were in the kitchen when I woke up. They were talking about something, but stop when they see me walking in.

"Good morning," I greet them, walking over to the fridge. "How was your date night?" I had gone to bed by the time they had gotten home.

I open the fridge and pull out a carton of orange juice.

I expect my parents to greet me back and tell me about their night. Instead they sat there, their hands around their mugs of coffee, looking at me with real concern. As soon as I see their faces, my immediate thought was that something bad has happened. I just didn't know what. My body freezes, not knowing if I could take any more bad news after what happened with Josh.

I put the carton of orange juice down on the counter before

I drop it.

"Mum, Dad, is everything okay?" I ask them. "Why are you looking at me like that?"

Dad removes his hand from his mug, and gestures to the chair beside him. "Can you sit down please, Emily? Your mother and I need to talk to you about something."

I obey Dad and sat down beside him. I look between my parents, waiting for them to speak.

"Your mother and I just want to see how you have been coping with Josh's death," Dad says. "You barely talk about what happened and we want to know if you're okay."

I look between my parents, unsure what to tell them. "I'm fine. Why?"

Mum and Dad look at each other before turning back to me.

"I was speaking to Lynn this morning," Mum says. "She has expressed some concern about you."

My body goes cold. They know. They know I have been seeing Josh.

"She said she saw you out on the patio last night," Mum goes on. "She heard you talking to yourself. It sounded like you were having a conversation with someone, but no one was there."

I sit there in silence, staring down at the table. I couldn't look at them and tell them what was going on with me. How could I tell them when I wasn't sure myself?

"Is there anything we should know about?" Mum reaches across the table and put her hand over mine. "Are you seeing things you shouldn't? Can you see dead people?"

I couldn't tell them. They will think I'm crazy. I'm not crazy!

I quickly came up with something to explain to my parents.

I couldn't tell them anything about my own insanity when I don't know myself. I don't want them to think I'm crazy when I know I'm not.

"Mum, Dad, no. I'm not seeing things that aren't there and I can't see dead people. I'm pretty sure it was all just a misunderstanding. I was on the phone with Haylie." The guilt for lying to my parents quickly builds up. I fidget with my hands, hoping my parents won't notice me lying or ask me more questions on what was going on. I can't answer them. Not right now.

My parents didn't say anything for a few minutes. Dad breaks the silence.

"Okay," he says. "But you know you can talk to us if something is bothering you, Emily. We will listen."

I nod. "Of course."

At the back of my mind, I heard a voice tell me to open up to my parents with what is going on. But I can't tell them. I just can't. I don't want my parents to worry about what is going on with me. They have enough to worry about themselves instead of wondering if their only child is seeing things that aren't meant to be there.

I'm fine.

Aren't I?

* * *

"Hey, so I was thinking maybe you could come over this afternoon to work on that English assignment together," Haylie says to me as we take a seat under our tree.

Homework was the last thing on my mind. "Sure. I haven't really started it yet. When is it due?"

"It has to be done by next Monday so the teachers can put together our final marks."

"I can't wait until we finish all our assignments. They're nothing but headaches." I especially couldn't wait until I no longer have to worry about maths anymore.

"Tell me about it."

We sit there in silence for a moment until Haylie turns to me, her face beaming.

"You will never guess what happened last night," she says.

"What?"

"Jensen and I went out, and he kissed me for the first time."

I don't respond to this straight away. I should be jumping up and down excitedly, cheering this experience on with my friend. But all I could think back was to that night with Josh, where we admitted our feelings to each other and we kissed for the first time. How I wish I could feel Josh's lips on mine again.

I force myself to smile so Haylie wouldn't think that I didn't care, because I did.

"That's great, Haylie." I twist my body around so I'm facing her, putting one leg up on the seat. "Tell me everything. What was the kiss like?"

Before Haylie had the chance to respond, Gabby walks over to us.

"You little bitch."

We turn to see her walking over to us with Samantha, Lake, Ron and Elliot. She stands in front of me, her hands on her hips and a frown upon her face, like she was about ready to kill someone.

"How dare you slap my boyfriend across his face last night!" Gabby scrolls at me.

I stare at Gabby, confused about why she was calling Lake

her boyfriend when they had broken up. And why would she care about me slapping him? If only she knew what he had tried to do to me, then she would understand.

"Your boyfriend?" Haylie was just as confused as I was. "I thought you and Lake broke up?"

"We did, but we got back together last night," Lake speaks up.

Even though I was not interested in him, this announcement still made my heart crumble. It was like he had been putting on an act all of this time, saying he no longer wanted to associate with Gabby and tell me how he feels towards me, only to go back to her. It was like I was never important to him. Just someone he could maybe use to make Gabby jealous. How could I be such a fool to think he would care about me?

Haylie scoffs. "Why doesn't that surprise me? I mean, Lake, you have been hitting on Emily as soon as you broke up with Gabby, and now you're back with her? Wow."

"We aren't talking to you, Haylie. So shut the hell up why don't you?" Gabby snaps.

Haylie sticks her middle finger up at her.

Gabby ignores her and turns to me. She crosses her arms across her chest, narrowing her eyes at me. "So? Are you going to tell me why you slapped him?" She gestures to Ron and Elliot. "Or should I get these two to beat you up so you will talk?"

I glance at Ron and Elliot, who both give me smirks. I hear Ron chuckle. No. I wasn't going to let those two bullied me like they would do with Josh. I glance around, looking for Josh, hoping he would appear. Could he do something to make them leave me alone?

But of course, Josh isn't here. He can't help me. I need to

do this on my own without him. I have stood up to these guys when they bullied Josh, and I can do it again for myself.

I turn back to Gabby who is waiting for my answer. Instead of explaining to her what happened, I say, "Why don't you ask Lake about it? I'm sure he can tell you everything. He was the one who came to my house in the first place." I turn to Haylie. "Come on, Haylie. Let's go."

Haylie and I get off the bench, but before we could walk away, Ron and Elliot grab my arms from either side. I try to break free, but my struggles make them grip me tighter so I couldn't escape. I wince.

"No, no," Elliot says. "You aren't going anywhere."

"Let her go!" Haylie tries to push them away, but Lake holds her back. Haylie tries to fight back. "Don't touch me!"

"Quiet, or I will hurt you," Lake threatens her, tightening his grip on her, making her wince.

Samantha just stands there with a huge grin on her face, like she was holding back a laugh on what her friends were doing to me and Haylie.

Gabby leans her face into mine. In a threatening tone, she says, "Tell me or I will do something you would regret for touching my boyfriend."

My body shivers at her threat. "What will you do?"

She shrugs. "I guess you will find out if you don't tell me."

I glance over at Haylie, who glances at me with worry. Lake has a smirk on his face. I frown at him. Does he really think he can get away with what he did last night and get his stupid girlfriend involve, making her do all of the threats because he is such a coward, or can't stand up to admit what he had done wrong?

I turn back to Gabby. "Lake tried to force himself onto me."

I tell her about how he came over to my house, checking up on me with the things she had said that day. Before he left, he wanted a glass of water, so I let him in. I leave out the details about me talking to Josh, and tell her how Lake had forced a kiss on me without my consent.

Haylie gasps. "You never mentioned to me this."

My eyes stay focus on Gabby instead of responding to my friend.

Gabby laughs, like I had told her one big joke. Of course she wasn't going to take this seriously. "That's not what Lake told me. He told me *you* went over to his house and tried to *kiss him*. When he refused to kiss you back, you slapped him."

I glance over at Lake, my heart sinking deep into my chest. His smirk is still on his face. Why would he lie like that? Why couldn't he man up and admit what he did wrong?

Gabby grabs my face, her nails digging into my skin as she turns my face towards her. "Hey, keep your eyes on me, not my boyfriend. I know you're mourning over Freak, but that doesn't mean you can steal my boyfriend just because yours decided to kill himself."

Her words pierced right through my heart. My eyes prickled with tears threatening to fall, but I did everything I could to hold them back. I couldn't cry in front of Gabby and her friends. She will call me weak. I couldn't believe Lake would go ahead and lie like that.

I wanted to open my mouth to say something back, but my mouth wouldn't open. If I did, I was sure I would burst into tears and wouldn't be able to control them once I let them go.

Gabby lets go of me and takes a step back. She held a finger up towards me. "You stay away from my boyfriend, you hear me? Don't let me warn you again."

I gulp, nodding slowly. It's not like I was planning to go anywhere near him anyway, but I'm sure he will be the one to disobey his girlfriend and come near me.

Gabby tells Ron and Elliot to let me go, and they do. Lake lets go of Haylie.

The bell rings before she can threat me with anything else.

"Have a great day, Emily." Gabby gives me a smirk before walking away. Her friends follow her.

Lake looks over his shoulder at me, giving me a sneer.

Haylie turns to me. "Are you okay, Emily?"

My eyes don't meet hers as my lip trembles. She walks over to me, hugging me tightly. I couldn't hold the tears back any longer. I sob loudly in her shoulder, and she rubs a hand up and down my back, soothing me.

"It's okay," she says, her voice instantly calming me. "Don't listen to her."

She pushes me gently off her, her hands sitting on my shoulders.

"It hurts, Haylie."

Haylie nods. "I know. Josh is my friend too, and it hurts what Gabby said too. Do you think you will be okay to be at school? We can skip if you want?"

I shake my head, wiping my eyes. "I'm okay. I will try not to let her get to me. And I'm sorry about not mentioning to you about last night with Lake. I should have told you."

Haylie gives me a small smile. She takes my hand. "Let's talk about this later and get to roll call."

* * *

Gabby's words about Josh killing himself stayed with me for the whole day. It was all I could think about. Each time I thought about it, the hole in my heart got bigger. Seeing Gabby around school didn't help. It made me angrier, hating myself for agreeing to go on that stupid camping trip. I should have told Josh no. I shouldn't have told him how I felt. Maybe, just maybe, he would still be here right now.

I was glad once school ended for the day, and I could be with Haylie for the rest of the afternoon. My English assignment was the least of my worries right now, but I had to try and distract myself the best I could.

Haylie and I sat on her bed with our books to work together. We had the house to ourselves since her father was still at work and her mother had taken her younger brother to soccer practice. Elijah was probably at work or at band practice. I try my best to concentrate on our assignment, but I couldn't stop thinking about Gabby or Lake.

After working on our assignments for an hour, I left to use the bathroom. I needed a break. There, I was able to be alone for a moment with my thoughts for the first time today. I stare at my reflection in the mirror for a long time. I wasn't sure what I was staring at or what I was looking for in my reflection. I just wanted to kick myself for thinking that these past two weeks I had been tricked into thinking that Lake Terra was a decent guy. Someone I could go to if I needed a shoulder to cry on. It was a trick all along.

I should have gone to Elijah instead when he asked me to. He knows me more than Lake does. He will listen. He wouldn't judge me.

"I am such a fool," I say to my reflection. "How could I believe for a second that Lake was interested in me or wanted to be my friend? I mean, I knew it was strange for him to start liking me all of a sudden, but I didn't expect him to push me into a relationship so quickly... That's if he even liked me at all."

A hand rests on my shoulder. "You aren't a fool, Emily."

I turn to him. "I feel like I am, Josh."

He shakes his head. "No, you're not."

He pulls me into a hug. We stand there for a while in each other's arms. I didn't want to let go of him at all.

"I wish I could stay in your arms forever, Josh, and not let go," I say.

"Maybe there is a way you can hold onto me forever and you would never have to let me go."

I pull away from him, staring at him and wondering what he meant by that. "What do you mean, Josh?"

Before Josh could answer me, a knock came from the door, follow by Haylie's voice.

"Emily, are you okay in there?" she asks me.

"Yeah, I'm fine," I reply back. I open the door.

"Are you sure you are okay?" Haylie asks me again, giving me a concern look. The exact same look my parents were giving me this morning. "Who were you talking to?"

"Nobody." I push pass her and headed back to her room.

Haylie follows me. "It didn't sound like nobody, Emily. It sounded like you were talking to someone whose name is Josh. And don't say you were talking on the phone because it's in my room. Yesterday when I went to get you after you ran out of class, I heard you talking to someone and that's how I knew you were hiding in the restrooms. Are you talking to Josh? Can you see him?"

I stop walking and turn to her. I wanted to lie, but Haylie would know if I am. Maybe I should tell her what is going on.

After all, she is my only friend now and she deserves the right to know.

I take a deep breath and come clean with her. "I have been seeing Josh."

Haylie looks a little confused. "Seeing him? How? Like as a spirit?"

I shake my head. "No. He's more like a hallucination."

Haylie stands there for a moment, her mouth slightly open. "A hallucination? You don't have schizophrenia or some other mental illness, do you?"

I shake my head. "No. I don't know why I can see him, but I know it's not schizophrenia or some other illness."

"Emily, you need to go and get yourself check out."

"No. Everyone will assume I'm crazy. I will be locked up."

"No, you won't be, Emily. Maybe you have another condition causing you to see Josh. You should check it out before it gets worse. Or maybe it's just grief causing this hallucination. You need to talk to someone to help you through this."

Haylie was right. I should get myself check out or talk to someone about the grief. But I'm sure I'm fine.

Chapter 24

My parents were waiting for me as soon as I walk through the front door. They call me into the kitchen. I find them sitting at the table, serious looks on their faces. It reminded me of this morning when they expressed their concerns about me.

Dad gestures to the chair next to him. "Take a seat, Emily. Your mother and I need to have a talk with you."

I listen, taking a chair next to Dad. "Am I in trouble?"

Mum shakes her head, giving me a small smile. "No, you aren't, sweetie. We just want to talk."

I'm afraid to know what they wanted to talk about. "I thought we spoke this morning? I told you guys that I'm coping fine."

Dad and Mum give each other a brief glance before turning back to me.

"We know, but we feel we need to discuss it again with you,"

Dad says.

"Emily, we need you to tell us the truth this time," Mum adds.

I look at them, not quite sure what they were getting at. "What truth?"

"The truth about what we were asking you about this morning," Dad says. "When we asked who you were talking to, you said you were talking on the phone to Haylie. Now that wasn't true, was it?"

I swallow hard. They know. How do they know I have been talking to Josh?

My mind races for a quick explanation, unsure if I should keep lying or confess the truth this time. I'm sure my parents wouldn't think I'm crazy if I tell them the truth, right? They will understand what I'm going through. Haylie did say the grief is most likely causing the hallucinations.

I decided to go with the lying. It was the only way I can stop having them from bombarding me with questions I don't want to answer. "I was talking to Haylie."

"No, you weren't!" Dad's voice rose, making me jump. He rarely ever raises his voice at me. "Tell us the truth, Emily."

Mum gives Dad a look as to tell him to calm down. She rests a hand on his shoulder. "Steve, please don't yell." She turns to me, giving me a small smile. "Emily, please. Tell us what is going on and what is bothering you. We know what you must be going through with what happened to Josh. Your father and I want you to know how we are here for you, and we will help you through this. Just tell us what is going on. Please."

I remain silence, unsure what I should tell my parents. I stare down at the table so I could avoid eye contact.

"Emily, we don't want you to feel you're in trouble," Dad

goes on to say when I don't say anything. "Your mother and I are worried about you. Lynn is worried about you. So are your friends."

I look up at Dad, unsure if I heard right. "Wait. What? Friends? I only have one friend and that's Haylie."

"Your friend Lake—"

"Lake?" I snicker. Was my dad being serious right now? I have *never* considered him as a friend, even when he was pretending to act all nice to me. I thought I could try, but let's face it. Lake and I were never meant to be friends. "Lake isn't my friend."

"Well, classmate then," he continues. Yeah, I barely count him as a classmate either. The word mate doesn't exactly describe how he has been treating me lately. "Lake was here not long ago, expressing concern about you. He said he has seen you talking to yourself yesterday."

"A lot of people talk to themselves," I say. "It doesn't mean anything."

But neither of my parents listened to what I had to say.

Dad resumes. "Once he left, your mother called Haylie to ask if she knew about your strange behaviour. She said she has heard you talking to someone who wasn't there twice."

I sat there, not knowing what to say. There was no use to keep lying. I might as well as spill the truth. After all, my parents were bound to find out about Josh. How could I think that I could keep this all a secret from them? Or from anyone?

"Is what Haylie told us the truth, Emily?" Mum asks me.

"I…" I look between my parents. "I have been seeing, Josh."

I wait for my parents to say I'm crazy, but they don't. They let the news sink in, giving me concern looks.

"Seeing Josh?" Dad asks. "How? Like hallucinating him?"

I nod. "Yes."

"How long have you been seeing him, Emily?" Mum wants to know.

"Just for a couple of days. I started seeing him the day after you gave me the car, and I drove up to Deighton Falls. I can't exactly explain how I started seeing him. He just appeared."

My parents sit there in silence for a few short minutes.

"Tomorrow your mother and I are going to look around for you to see someone," Dad says. "We want to help you get better. We will also book you into seeing the school counsellor."

I look between my parents. "You think I'm crazy?"

Mum shakes her head. "No, Emily. No one is saying you're crazy."

"I'm sure you think I am. Why don't you go ahead and say it? I'm crazy. I'm turning into Josh. That's what Gabrielle Casey at school keeps saying."

"Calm down, Emily," Dad says. "We aren't saying you're crazy. We want you to get help so you can get better. You just need to talk with a grief counsellor who can help you get through with Josh's death."

I stand up, my chair scraping across the kitchen floor. I slam the palm of my hand on the table. "Bull crap."

Dad frowns at me. In a firm voice, he warns, "Emily, don't use that language."

"Then don't lie to me when you say you don't think I'm crazy!" I shout. "I know that's what you're thinking! It's what some people thought about Josh when he used to hallucinate."

Dad stands up. "Emily, I need you to calm down. Your mother and I aren't thinking anything. We are thinking that you're our daughter and we want you to get the help you need to get through this. And I don't know who these people you're preferring to, but your mother and I definitely didn't think Josh was crazy when he began hallucinating. He had a mental health illness that caused him to see and hear things, and that is not his fault. If you have something similar to Josh, we want to be able to help you, Emily. If it isn't psychosis you have, then perhaps its grief."

I look between my parents, unsure if I want to believe them. They think I'm crazy, don't they? Will they even send me to counselling? Or will I be sent away somewhere to get the help I need? I didn't want to be sent away to anywhere. And I'm pretty sure I will be fine if I don't talk to someone professionally with what is going on with me. I can grieve through Josh's death without anyone's help.

You aren't fine, Emily, I tell myself. *You need help even if you think you don't.*

I look over at where Josh stood in between the door frame. He stares back at me, looking at me with worry.

You shouldn't be seeing Josh, a voice tells me. *It's not normal, Emily. You do need help.*

I turn back to my parents. "I'm not crazy."

"Honey, we aren't saying you are," Mum says. "We just want you to talk to someone with how you're feeling. Someone who can help you get through this grief. And if you're dealing with something more than grief, we want to make sure you get the help you need."

I knew my parents meant well, and they wanted what was best for me. But in the back of my mind, this voice kept telling me that I'm fine and I will get through this without anyone's help. Yet, I knew the inner voice was wrong and I don't know why I was listening to it when I'm fully aware of the help I needed.

I glance over at Josh again and that's when I lose it. I sit back down on the chair and burst into tears. I fold my arms on the table and bury my face in them, sobbing loudly.

Dad rubs a hand along my back, soothing me. "It's okay, sweetie."

I shake my head while my face was still buried in my arms. "It's not okay. *I'm* not okay. I miss Josh. I miss him every day. I wish I could go back in time to save him. Without him here, I feel I'm slowly losing myself."

"You aren't losing yourself, Emily. You're mourning someone you care deeply about, and it's okay that you feel this way."

I shake my head. "I am losing myself. I'm not sane. I can see Josh. I can feel him. I can talk to him. I shouldn't be able to do any of that. I don't know what's wrong with me!"

Mum's hand reaches across the table and rests it on my wrist. "Emily, look at me."

I obey my mum, and look up at her, my face wet with salty tears.

"Everything is going to be okay. Don't think you are losing your mind, because you aren't. You have gone through a tragic event, and it's okay for you to grieve. Hallucinating Josh doesn't mean you're crazy. I'm pretty sure there is an explanation for all of this. You can get through this."

I nod, wiping my eyes. "I'm going to go up to my room. I need to be alone."

Mum lets go of my wrist. "Of course, sweetie."

I get up from the table and headed up to my room. I lie down on my bed and stare up at the ceiling. So many things were running through my mind, and I didn't know what I wanted to do about this whole situation. Accepting help is the right thing to do, so why wasn't I accepting it?

"Emily?"

I turn on my side and see Josh standing beside my bed.

"Are you okay?"

I nod. "I'm fine, Josh. I just need some time to myself to think everything over."

Josh steps forward and takes my hand. "Come on. Let's get out of here."

Chapter 25

Josh suggests we drive up to Deighton Falls Campgrounds. I snuck out of the window with him, not wanting my parents to know where I was going. I have never snuck out of the house after arguing with my parents before, but right now I just wanted time to myself to think. And getting out of the house is what I needed to do right now. I know my parents mean well and they wanted to do what they could to help me. I shouldn't be mad at them for that.

Putting on the radio, I try to shut my thoughts out with the music. It helps a little, but I still can't help but wonder what is going to happen once I start going to therapy.

It's dark once I get to the campgrounds. It's empty and I almost didn't want to get out of the car and into the pitched black. I grab my phone, ignoring the three missed calls and texts from my parents, turning on the torch app. I shiver briefly, looking around the campsite. I walk over to where we had set up camp. How did everything go wrong that night?

I stand next to the campfire, burnt wood and ashes from the last person who used it. I remember Josh and I sitting here, talking, laughing, eating, singing songs on his guitar and what aches my heart the most, sharing our first kiss. I also remember the days we would come here with our parents. Now all of those memories seem like so long ago. That's all I have. Just memories of Josh. I will never get to experience new things with him, or hold him, talking about our future and laugh over jokes.

A lump forms in my throat as tears threaten to fall again.

Josh stands beside me, putting his hand on my shoulder. "It's okay, Emily."

I shake my head. My voice chokes on my words as I burst into tears. I fell to my knees and bury my face in my hands. "It's not okay, Josh. You aren't here anymore. I will never get to see you again."

Josh kneels beside me. "What are you talking about, Em? Of course you can see me again. You are seeing me right now."

I force myself to move my hands away from my face and look at Josh, wiping my eyes. He gives me a small smile as to tell me that everything is going to be okay. How is everything going to be okay? Nothing will ever be the same again! "You're just a hallucination, Josh. I'm not supposed to see you. I don't understand why I can see you."

Josh is taken aback. He knows what I said is true, but doesn't say anything. He pulls me close to him and wraps his arms around me. I sob into his shoulder, glad that there was no one around except for us. He rubs a hand up and down my arm, instantly soothing me, and rests his chin on my head.

We sit still for a while until my phone rings. I pull away

from him, wiping my eyes, and check to see who was calling me. Hailey's name flashes across the screen. I accept the call. No doubt my parents have contacted her to see if I was with her, and now she was calling me to see where I was. I didn't want to talk to her, but I knew I had to let someone know that I was alright.

I answer the call, putting her on speaker, but I don't say anything.

"Emily?" Haylie's voice comes over the phone in a worried tone. "Are you there?"

"I am," I choke out.

"Are you okay? Where are you? Your parents said you had walked out of the house without telling anyone where you are going."

"Don't tell her where we are," Josh tells me. "Let us be alone without anyone coming to find us."

The words were on the tip of my tongue, and I wanted to tell her where I was, even when Josh was telling me not to. I don't know why he was telling me to say it.

I burst into tears.

"Emily? Are you okay?"

"I'm fine," I choke out over my sobs.

"You're not. Where are you?" She pauses, waiting for me to tell her. When I don't answer her, she guesses where I could be from my silence. "Are you at Deighton Falls Campgrounds?"

I don't answer, sobbing hard.

"Hold on, Emily. I'm coming for you."

I wanted to tell her not to come, that there is no point for her to come here, but my mouth wouldn't move. Haylie hangs up. I stare at the screen even though the tears blocked my vision. I cry for what seems like for hours. My phone rings again, but I don't check to see who is calling. It's no doubt my parents calling now. I can't talk to them right now.

"Why does this hurt so much?" I say to Josh.

He puts a hand on my shoulder. "You are going to be okay, Em."

I shake my head. "I don't feel okay."

I'm broken. I don't feel I can go on without Josh. It's so hard to move on without him. How do I stop feeling like this?

I push Josh's hand away and then curl up on the ground beside the burned out campfire. I shiver from the cold. I should start a fire to keep me warm or even get back into the car, but I can't move my body. I want to just lie here, forget about the world around me. If I couldn't have Josh here with me, how would I be able to go on without him? Nothing is ever going to be the same without him. I cry until there are no tears left.

"Emily, talk to me," Josh says after a long time.

"I can't talk right now. You're not real, Josh."

"What are you talking about, Em? I am real."

I force myself to sit up and look up at him. He is sitting here looking right at me. My phone may not be a great source of light, but I could see him. He has this worried expression, wanting to help me the best way he could but there wasn't anything he could do. He was dead. He was just a hallucination in which I shouldn't even be seeing. But I am.

"You're dead, Josh," I tell him. He's taken back from my words. "You're a hallucination. I'm not even supposed to be seeing you."

"But you're seeing me."

"And I don't know why." I cover my face with my hands. "There is something wrong with me."

I hear him moving in the dirt as he comes closer to me. He

moves my hands away from my face so I'm looking at him.

"There is nothing wrong with you," he says.

I shake my head. He doesn't get it. He just doesn't get it. "If there is nothing wrong, then I wouldn't be seeing you."

Josh reaches out and strokes my cheek. "It's alright, Emily."

I push Josh off me and stand up. He gets to his feet as well.

"No, don't you get it, Josh? It's *not* alright. *I'm* not alright. You're dead, and I can see you. There is something wrong with me. I thought I could hide it from everyone and just pretend that I'm okay, but clearly I'm not. I need help."

"I will help you."

"No, Josh. You can't help me at all. How can you help me? You're dead. Ever since you died, I can't cope without you. I'm terrified that I'm losing my own insanity right now."

He looks at me sadly, and I almost feel bad for saying these things to him. I shouldn't though. He isn't real.

"Is that what this is about, Em?" Josh says. "Is it about me being dead?"

I close my eyes. I want Josh to leave. I don't want to see him anymore. He isn't real. He is a hallucination. It was great having him here to comfort me, but now it's scaring me with how much I'm losing my mind. Maybe I couldn't see what was happening before, but with the things Haylie and my parents have been saying, I know I need help even if I don't want to admit it.

Without saying anything, I turn my back to him. Using my phone as a guide, I make my way across the campsite towards the trail leading to the lookout. I don't look back to see if he is following me or not. I don't want him to follow. I just want to be left alone with my own thoughts and not have him part of it.

I almost trip on something in my path, and manage to correct my balance. The last thing I needed was to injure myself badly and having to wait for hours to receive help. Something snaps on the ground somewhere around me. I stop, looking around into the darkness of the woods.

"Hello?" I call out to nothing. Then I instantly regret calling out because if this was a horror film, I would have just gotten myself killed.

But it's silent. Not a single thing stirring in the night of the bush. It was just me out here and maybe animals that wouldn't care that I was here. I stand there for a moment, listening to anything just in case I was wrong.

"Josh?" I call out.

Of course there is no answer. Josh isn't here.

I scan around me one last time with my phone, and then keep walking down to the lookout. I soon hear the waterfall. And when I get there, an ache in my heart forms. I walk slowly towards the lookout, wondering what could have gone through Josh's mind when he took these exact steps. Was I even part of his thoughts as he escaped from whatever his delusions or hallucinations were telling him to run from?

Once again I stand at the railing. I couldn't see the waterfall, but I could hear it. I close my eyes, resting my hands on the railing while still holding my phone.

"Why did you do it, Josh?" I whisper to myself.

"I'm sorry if I did, Emily."

I jump at the sound of his voice. I spin around to see him walking over to me.

"I explain why I did it," he says.

I shake my head. "But still, you didn't have to leave, Josh."

"I had to."

"No, you didn't, you bastard!" I shove him hard in the chest once he reached me. I didn't want him to come any closer to me.

I couldn't figure things out with him here.

Josh looks at me, confused. "Why are you so mad at me, Em? I explained to you what had happened."

I scoff. Did he really want to know why I was mad at him?

"I'm mad at you, Josh, because you didn't fight. You listened to the voices. It's like you didn't care how I would feel. I have been beside you long before you were diagnosed with schizophrenia. Sometimes you spoke to me about your hallucinations, and I would help you through whatever they told you. Like when Aspen told you not to get up onto the stage with Elijah's band. I told you to focus on just me and you got through it fine. And if the voices were bothering you that night, you could have woken me up, Josh. You could have woken me up and I would have done something to help you."

Josh shakes his head. "Even if I could have woken you up, there's nothing you could ever do to help me get through this. I was always going to hear voices or see things that aren't there. The medication I take didn't always helped me. If they couldn't help me, how could you have helped me, Emily?"

I shrug. "I don't know, Josh. You're right. I couldn't stop you from hearing voices or seeing things. But I could always be there for you. That's all I ever wanted to do. I wanted to be there for you. What hurts the most about you leaving me behind, is that you admitted how you felt towards me. I have hidden how I felt towards you for a long time, scared to tell you how I felt. When you kissed me, it felt like this most amazing thing in the world. It washed away the fear of how I thought you might act if you knew I liked you more than just a friend. Finding you the next morning at the bottom of the cliff was the worst day of my life that I don't think I would ever forget. It crushed me, Josh."

Josh stands there, unsure what to say. I waited for him to

say something, but it seemed like he just wanted me to do the talking.

So I carry on.

"For the past few days, I have wondered to myself what would have happened to us if you hadn't died. I imagine what my life would be with you, all the things we had planned to do together. Didn't any of that matter for you when you stood here?"

Josh looks from me to the railing and then back at me. "I swear I wasn't meant to jump."

"But you did. Before Davis stopped you, snapping you out of whatever voices that were controlling you."

"I·slipped, Emily."

"And you wouldn't have slipped if you hadn't climbed over the rail!"

I threw my phone at him, needing to throw something in the frustration and anger that I had felt. The pain in my chest tightens, and I say the words I don't want to say, but they slip off my tongue so naturally.

"I hate you!" I scream.

My phone drops to the ground with a thud. I have no idea where it was or how damaged it was. The torch light goes out on it, and I'm standing in complete darkness. The moon wasn't even out, hiding behind clouds, stopping me from seeing anything.

"I hate you!" I scream again into the night.

Was Josh still standing there? I don't know. I can't see him in the darkness. I want him to leave. I don't want to see him.

I sit down on the ground beside the railing, curling up in a ball. The tears are back, and I'm sobbing hard.

"I hate you for leaving me," I say this time in a soft voice.

* * *

I don't know how long it has been since I had curled up near the railing of the lookout. The tears have dried, and I shiver in the darkness. I should get up and head back to my car, but I can't move from this spot. I have no idea if Josh was still around. I haven't even looked up to see if he was here or hear him speak. I was glad because it meant I could be alone with my own thoughts.

It's all quiet except for the waterfall. Somewhere in the distance I hear an owl. But other than that, I'm sitting here in complete silence.

Well, it was quiet until I hear voices.

"She's over here!" a male voice calls out to someone.

I don't look up to see who was coming over, but I hear their feet running over to me on the pavement

"Emily!"

It's Elijah. He kneels down beside me, gently putting a hand under my chin and lifts my head up. He puts his phone down with the torch facing up. I can see the worry in his eyes. I have known Elijah for a long time since Haylie and I became friends in pre-school, and I don't think I have ever seen him so worried about me.

"Are you okay, Emily?" he asks me.

I nod slowly.

"You're freezing!"

He takes off his jacket and puts it around my shoulders. Haylie joins us.

"Oh my gosh, Emily!" She threw her arms around me. "I was so worried. Your parents called to ask where you were. And when I learned you were here, I was worried what you might do. I told Elijah where you were and he decided to come with me to find you."

I rest my head on Haylie's shoulder.

"I'm crazy," I say. "I think I'm losing my mind. I can see Josh."

Haylie makes me look up at her. "Hey, it's okay, Em. You aren't crazy."

"But I must be if I could see him."

Elijah tucks a strand of my hair behind my ear. "It's just grief, Emily. Grief can make you hallucinate. It doesn't make you crazy."

"Why don't we get you to the car and take you home?" Haylie suggests.

I nod, knowing that home will be a good idea right now.

Haylie and Elijah helped me off the ground, walking me back to the campsite. Haylie finds my phone on the ground before we leave the lookout. The screen is cracked, but it's still working.

"I'm glad you're alright, Emily," Haylie says. "You really scared me when your parents called to say you had walked out of the house, wondering if I had seen you. I told them not since you had left my place."

"I'm sorry," I say. "I didn't mean to scare anyone. I just panicked when my parents suggested I receive counselling when I was caught out for talking to a hallucination. I didn't want to be called crazy."

"No one is going to call you crazy," Elijah says. "You're going through a rough time right now. You just lost someone very important to you. You're going to get help to get you through this. Everything is going to be okay."

We reach the car and Haylie opens the passenger side door while Elijah helps me inside, putting on my seat belt. He takes his jacket from me and puts it on him.

"Are you okay now?" he asks.

I nod slowly. "I'm okay."

I think.

He gives me a small smile. "That's good." He turns to his sister. "Get her home and I will meet you there."

Elijah closes the door and heads back to his car while Haylie gets into the driver's seat, starting the car.

I rest my head on the window. When I do, I spot Josh standing there, just a few feet from the car.

"I'm sorry, Emily," he says, his eyes filled with sadness. "I was never meant to hurt you."

But you did hurt me, I say to myself.

* * *

As soon as we pull up outside of my home, with Elijah pulling up behind, the front door swings open. Mum is the first person to run down the lawn with Dad following her. She embraces me as soon as she gets to me, her face wet with tears.

"Oh, thank goodness you're alright, Emily," Mum says.

"I'm so sorry for running away like I did," I say, resting my head on Mum's shoulder. "I didn't mean to worry anyone. I panicked with what was going on."

Mum strokes my back. "It's okay, sweetie. Your father and I are just glad you're alright."

Dad comes up to me and Mum pulls away. He pulls me into a hug.

"Everything is going to be alright," he says.

Mum thanks Haylie and Elijah for finding me. Before they go, they hug me goodbye. Haylie tells me she will call me tomorrow and then gets into her brother's car. My parents walk me inside where Mum decides to make us hot chocolate so we could settle down on the couch and talk. I didn't want to talk, mostly wanting to be by myself, but it was nice to be able to be with my parents for the rest of the evening.

Chapter 26

I stay home from school the next day. Mum takes the day off from work to be with me, and is on the phone first thing in the morning as soon as the office is open to schedule an appointment for me to see a therapist. I wasn't able to see one until Tuesday. In the meantime, my parents wanted me to rest for the day while I take some time off from school, and rest over the weekend before going back to school on Monday. Haylie said she will be over later to drop off homework for me.

Mum wouldn't let me mope about in my room, even though all I wanted was to be alone. So she made me sit out in the lounge room where she could keep an eye on me while she cleaned up the house, and also worked on some things for work. I sat on the couch, mixing my time up with a bit of television and then working on some unfinished homework.

When Haylie comes around in the afternoon with my

homework, she comes up with me to my room.

"How are you feeling today?" she asks me, setting my homework down on my desk.

I sit down on my bed. "Okay, I guess."

"I'm just glad you're okay."

"I am too. I still don't understand why Josh did it. I keep asking myself every time why. He told me he wasn't going to jump, that something was after him, and he realised that he should go back to me. Then he slipped before he could climb back over the rail. But I realised last night that I probably never even had that conversation with him. That it was probably all just in my head."

Haylie gives me a small smile. "It's probably your brain telling you what you would like to hear. None of us is ever going to know what really went through Josh's head. He has been fighting demons, and I know he was never meant to hurt any of us."

"In a letter he wrote me he said he felt like he was a burden on me because of his illness. I don't know why he would think that."

"You're never going to know why he would think that. None of us ever will. He could be fighting with something that's more than just thinking he was a burden. He was being bullied by Ron and Elliot, as well as Gabby. They could have said something to him. You don't know. He may have written a letter to you, explaining why he did this, but he probably never told you what was really going through his mind."

I nod, knowing Haylie was right. I just wish Josh could have opened up more, telling me things so I could try and help him. If I couldn't, at least I could be there for him to show my support.

Haylie joins me and pulls me into a hug. "You know I will always be here for you when you need to talk. I may not have the same close relationship you and Josh had, but I will help you in anywhere I can. You can count on me."

I pull away from her and smile for the first time since my breakdown yesterday. "Thanks, Haylie."

"If you're feeling up to it, Jensen and I are going to the movies tonight. You're welcome to join us."

I nod. Going to the movies might help me feel better. "I would love to come."

Haylie returns a smile. "Great. Jensen and I will come by at six to pick you up."

* * *

It's almost six when someone knocks on the door. I kiss my parents goodbye where Mum was putting the final touches on dinner for her and Dad. While Mum cooked, Dad and I set the table for the two of them.

"You have a good time at the movies, alright?" Dad says, handing me some money for the movie and snacks.

"I will," I answer, putting the money in my purse. "I don't know what time we will be finish."

"Just text us when you're on your way home," Mum says. "And don't stay out too late. You're also welcome to stay the night with Haylie. Let us know if you are."

I answer okay, and then head towards the front door. I open it. But it wasn't Haylie who was standing there.

"Elijah, what are you doing here?" I look behind him, expecting to see his sister, but she is nowhere around. "Are you coming to the movies with us?"

He shakes his head. "I wish. No, I'm actually on my way to band practice, and I thought I would stop by. I just wanted to check up on you to see how you are. Haylie told me how you are, but I thought it would be nice to come by myself to see you."

I smile. "Well, thanks, Elijah. I appreciate that. I'm okay. I'm not feeling one hundred percent, but I'm okay."

He returns the smile. "That's good to hear. Well, I better go before Haylie gets here. She doesn't know that I was stopping by to see you. I will see you around."

"Thanks for stopping by. Have fun with band practice."

"I will." He turns and heads to his car on the street.

I watch him leave and then sat on the front steps until Jensen pulls up in his car with Haylie. She waves at me and I get up, walking towards them.

Tonight I'm not going to let Josh's death get to me. Tonight I'm going to spend time with Haylie and her boyfriend. Everything is going to be alright.

Epilogue

TEN MONTHS LATER

I stare at my reflection in the mirror backstage. I take a few deep breaths and tell myself I can do this. It's for Josh. If he was here, he would be so proud of me.

A knock came from the door of my dressing room.

"Come in," I call out.

The door opens and I turn to see Haylie stepping into the room.

"Hey," she says with a smile. "Are you ready? It's almost time."

My stomach twists into knots and I almost want to throw up. I wonder if this is how Josh felt when he was asked to join Breaking Summer on the stage.

"I can't believe I'm doing this," I say.

Haylie walks over to me. "You're going to do fine out there. Josh would be so thrilled to know his song is going to be heard worldwide. And I don't think he could ask a better person to sing it for him."

I smile, knowing she was right. I could picture Josh standing in the front row of the stage, peering up at me, beaming, just like I had done when he was offered to sing at Breaking Summer's first gig. "But I'm not going to be the only one singing it."

Haylie nods. "I'm sure he will be honoured that you and Elijah will be singing it together."

Six months ago, Breaking Summer had scored their first record deal with Mad Star Records. The band held a small party to celebrate their deal. The party was also the first thing I had gone to since Josh's death. I didn't want to go at first, but Haylie managed to encourage me to get out there.

I had been doing well with my counselling, where I had gone to see someone once a week for two months before she decided to make it every fortnight as soon as I began coping better from Josh's death. For the rest of the school year, I tried my best to avoid Lake and Gabby, as well as their group of friends, doing everything I could to ignore their nasty comments until graduation in September. It was hard graduating, knowing I was never going to be able to share this day with Josh or attend the school formal. But Haylie had given me a heart locket with a picture of him inside, which I wear every day, having Josh close to my heart.

By December, I decided to stop the counselling services. With the new year approaching fast, I wanted to start fresh as I prepare for university at the end of January, where I was going to study mental health, maybe someday become a counsellor or a mental health worker. I had always dreamed of becoming a teacher, but with what happened to Josh I decided I wanted to help people.

The night of Breaking Summer's party, I approached Elijah. I would see him every now and again whenever I visit Haylie, always checking up on me to make sure I'm okay. I tell him about the recording Josh had made for *These Voices*. The other day when I was listening to it, the song gave me an idea, and I knew Elijah was the one person who I could trust with it.

"I was wondering if you would like to put that song on your album," I said. "I want to do it in honour of him."

I had thought about it for a long time, wanting the song kept between Josh and I. But then I thought the song could help others out there who could be struggling with their own schizophrenia. Josh would be thrilled if he had the opportunity to record any of the songs he had written.

Elijah smiled. "Of course. I would love to record it for him. I will let you make the decisions for this song."

I beamed, restraining myself from jumping up and down. "Thank you so much, Elijah. This means so much to me."

The next day after the party I went over to Haylie's and sat in the garage that was converted into a recording studio for Elijah. I played the recording Josh had left me. I didn't understand music, and I have no idea if Josh ever wrote out the notes to the song. But Elijah managed to learn the chords to it. The two of us worked on the song for days before his band was due to record some songs for their album. It was nice with just the two of us working on it. Keeping his word, he let me have full control on the song. He played around with the recording and I let him know what I thought of the sound, and what I thought the song was lacking. We kept at it until the song sounded perfect, ready for his band to record it.

One afternoon I was singing the song softly to myself. I didn't know Elijah had walked in and heard me after he stepped out to get us a drink, not until he spoke.

"You have a nice voice."

I jumped at the sound of his voice. "Thanks." I bit my lip, blushing. "I didn't hear you coming in."

He chuckled, sitting down next to me and hands me a glass of water. "Can you sing it again?"

I wasn't much of a singer, and I tried not to sing in public, except when I was around Josh. Occasionally, I sang with Haylie too, but never for anyone else.

"Pretend I'm not here," he said.

I sing the chorus. "*These voices are all that I can hear. These voices tell me things I don't want to hear...*"

"*Please take me by the hand,*" Elijah joined in.

"*Tell me that everything is going to be alright,*" we sung together, our voices forming well with the melody. "*Because tonight the only voice I want to hear is yours.*"

Elijah and I stared at each other for a long time, like we suddenly realised something we had never known before. The feeling gave me butterflies just thinking about it.

He clicked his fingers. "That's it. We should record this song together."

He turned to his computer and started fiddling around with it. "Okay. Let's sing that again. I want to see how this version goes."

I suddenly felt the need to go and hide from the world. "I don't sing."

He turned to me. "Emily, your voice is beautiful." My heart fluttered when he said this. "This song will sound even more special if you sang it with me. I think Josh would like that."

"So you want this to be like a duet?"

"No, not a duet. Your voice would sound good as backup in this. Let's try this out, and see if it could be a duet. You decide what you think should happen with the song."

Elijah recorded us singing just the chorus. When he played it back, I got goosebumps.

"It sounds perfect," I said.

"It does. So, do you think we could record it like this?"

"Only the chorus. I don't want to sing the whole song."

Elijah smiled. "We will record it like that, then."

The day we went to Mad Star Records to record the track, I felt like this whole experience was surreal. I never thought that my voice will be on the track of a song. Walking through the recording studio I imagine Josh for a moment, wondering what it would be like if he had the chance to record his own album. I imagine him being excited and nervous. And I wished he had the chance to do this as well. Recording this song was a way of living his dream, even if he wasn't the one who sings it.

We spent a few hours recording the song, making sure every part of it sounded perfect.

When the producer called for a break after we recorded it, Elijah and I stayed in the recording booth while two members of the band went to get coffee for everyone, a tea for me, while the other two went outside for a cigarette.

"Thank you so much for this opportunity," I told him.

He smiled, putting his guitar aside. "It's no problem at all. Josh will be happy."

I returned the smile. "He will."

Elijah and I stared at each other for a long time. The butterflies I felt the first time we sang the chorus had returned.

"Can I kiss you, Emily?" he asked.

My heart skipped a beat when he said this. It had been six months since Josh had passed away, and I hadn't thought of another guy since then. Also, Elijah was Haylie's brother. Would she even want us to be together? I do know one thing about Haylie, and she would want me to be happy. Even if it means I'm happy with her brother.

I nodded. "You can kiss me."

Elijah slowly stepped forward tucking my hair behind my ear, resting his hand on my cheek and kissed me. The kiss was soft and slow, sending all kinds of sensations throughout my body. For the first time in the last six months, I was happy.

Now as I walk through backstage with Haylie, my nerves are getting the better of me.

I stand at the side of the stage, waiting for Elijah to call me on. The band finishes a song and then while the other band members take a sip of water, Elijah spoke to the audience.

"This next song is a special one," Elijah says. "It was written by my sister's and girlfriend's friend, who had sadly passed away. Ten months ago, when we got our first gig at a club, my sister Haylie comes to me and says, 'Elijah, you know my friend, Josh?' 'Yeah.' 'He plays the guitar and talks about being a musician someday. He is a little shy about performing in front of an audience, but I think he would be able to perform up on the stage with you.' So the band and I allowed him to have the set to himself for a few minutes. He sang this song he had written about his schizophrenia. Six months ago, my girlfriend, Emily, approaches me about the song, asking if I could record it in honour of him. So we recorded it. This next song is dedicated to Joshua Harman. This is *These Voices*."

The crowd breaks out in a cheer. Elijah glances my way, giving me a smile, and I return it. He starts to play the song.

When the chorus comes in, I walk onto the stage with a microphone, singing. My heart pounds rapidly against my chest as the audience cheers me on. I stand beside Elijah, our voices coming together as we sing the chorus.

This is the first time we are singing this song live in front of an audience. And as we finish the song, the crowd cheering, for the first time in ten months I feel like my heart is whole. I can almost hear Josh saying how proud he is of me.

And I'm proud of myself too.

Australia
Lifeline
DIAL: 13 11 14
http://lifeline.org.au

Suicide Call Back Service
DIAL: 1300 659 467
http://suicidecallbackservice.org.au

Headspace
DIAL: 1800 650 890
http://headspace.org.au

Kids Helpline
DIAL: 1800 55 1800
http://kidshelpline.com.au/kids

ReachOut
http://au.reachout.com

New Zealand
Youthline
DIAL: 0800 376 633 OR FREE TEXT 234
http://www.youthline.co.nz

Need to Talk?
DIAL OR FREE TEXT 1737
http://www.1737.org.nz

The Lowdown
FREE TEXT 5626
http://thelowdown.co.nz

United Kingdom
Samaritans
DIAL: 116123 (free)
http://www.samaritans.org

Childline
DIAL: 0800 1111 (free)
http://www/childline.org.uk

United States
Crisis Text Line
If you are in crisis, reach out for help. Text HOME to 741741
http://www.crisistextline.org
Free, 24/7, confidential

National Suicide Prevention Lifeline
DIAL: 1-800-273-8255
http://www.suicidepreventionlifeline.org

Canada
Kids Help Phone
DIAL: 1-800-668-6868 (Kids Help Phone)
http://www.kidshelpphone.ca

Thursday's Child
DIAL: (818) 831-1234
http://www.thursdayschild.org
For bullying, eating disorders, self-injury, suicidal ideation,
sexual assault, etc.
24/7 and confidential for children, teens and young adults

Acknowledgements

I can't believe that this story has finally been published. I honestly never really thought I would ever see this story in print. I wrote this back in 2010, and I remember wanting this to be the first book I ever publish. But I'm so glad that I waited to published it because what I didn't know about schizophrenia then, over the years of researching I gathered the information with what I have learned, and added it into this story. This story has been the hardest one I have ever written, and the constant research I had done to get a clear idea with what could be going through Josh's head. Honestly, I was so afraid of publishing this that I never really thought I would ever get it out there. But I reminded myself to what made me so passionate about the project.

The idea of the story came to me in a dream. I didn't think I could write it, but I wrote a blurb to what I saw in my dream, and I began writing Josh's and Emily's story. This story has been an emotional ride, but it's finally done!

Thank you to my sister Jennifer, who constantly put up with me talking about this story so much when I first wrote it. Thank you to my mum for being the toughest woman I know, helping my brother, sister and I to understand and to be patient about mental health with my dad's bipolar. It has never been easy for you to hold us all together.

Thank you to Leonie Rhule for listening to me go on about

this story while I was rewriting and editing it. My writing slump has not been easy for me during this pandemic, and you have been there listening to me as I try my best with keeping on track with my writing.

Thank you also to Jennifer Niven, who I had met a few years ago while volunteering at the Sydney Writer's Festival, for giving me tips on writing a story about mental health. Your tips had helped me with rewriting this story and making it the best that I can, and I really appreciate it.

Thank you to my editor, Emily. You have done a great job with helping me draft this story in the best way I could.

About the Author

Jessica Madden was born and raised in Sydney, Australia. She began writing stories since the age of eight. When she was nine she realise that she wanted to be a writer more than anything in the world. In her late teens she started writing her stories up onto online communities. She was recommended by a friend to check out Wattpad, an online writing community for anyone to share, vote, read and upload stories.

When she is not writing, Jessica can be found being lost in a good book.

You can follow her on Twitter and Instagram **@JessicaCMadden**

Also by Jessica Madden

Right Here Waiting For You
The Jet Lag Diaries
Silent Love
Chasing The Storm

I Wasn't Supposed To Fall For You series
I Wasn't Supposed To Fall For You
It's All Because Of You

With You series
One Whole Night With You
Every Moment With You